Secrets of the Sorcerers

A Quest Fantasy

Chronicles of the Library of Sorcery

Secrets of the Sorcerers
A Quest Fantasy

Chronicles of the Library of Sorcery

Joan Marie Verba

FTL Publications
Minneapolis, Minnesota

FTL Publications
P O Box 22693
Minneapolis, MN 55345-0363
www.ftlpublications.com
mail@ftlpublications.com

Cover designed by Getcovers

Printed in the United States of America

ISBN 978-1-936881-76-5

Acknowledgments

I wish to extend my sincere thanks to the members of my critique group, Elizabeth Rowan Keith, Eleanor Dorn, Ted Schoep, and P.C. Hodgell, for their valuable advice and encouragement as I wrote this novel.

About the Author

Joan Marie Verba is an autistic author, publisher, and web developer with a bachelor's degree in physics. She was an associate instructor of astronomy for one year. She has worked as a computer programmer, web developer, editor, publisher, and social media manager. An experienced writer, she is the author of fiction and nonfiction books plus numerous short stories and articles. Her novels have received the Mom's Choice Award® and the Scribe Award. She is a member of the Science Fiction and Fantasy Writers Association and the International Association of Media Tie-in Writers.

To find out more about Joan, or to sign up for her newsletter, go to her website at https://joanmarieverba.com.

Prologue

Marlys had sunk into a deep, sweet dream of home when hands jerked her out of bed. She struggled to get her footing as the abductors, one on each side, hustled her out the door of the training house. Getting her breath, she shouted, "Help! Elspeth!" but there was no response from within. Outside, as she scrambled to keep up with her captors, she realized that these were Elspeth's other apprentice sorcerers, Janna and Kelsie, who she had only met that morning. Both were only one year older than Marlys, who was sixteen.

"What are you doing? Where are you taking me?"

No answer.

By the light of the full moon, Marlys could see they were headed toward the edge of the clearing, toward the woods. Dry branches had been piled next to a wooden post. When they got there, Janna shoved Marlys's back against the post as Kelsie pulled her arms back and tied them with leather thongs.

"Why are you doing this? I haven't done anything!"

Janna and Kelsie only giggled. They stepped away from the post. Janna kindled a flame and set the branches on fire.

Marlys gasped and flinched, straining at her bonds. "What do you want?"

"We want to see you burn, of course," Kelsie said blandly.

"Help! Help! Elspeth!" Surely the sorcerer could hear? How soundly did she sleep?

"Help, help," mocked Janna, and Kelsie laughed.

"Please! I'll do anything! Just let me go!"

"We don't want anything from you," Kelsie sneered.

Already smoke made Marlys cough. The flames grew each moment; they would reach her legs soon.

With an effort, she held her breath and thought. She knew some household spells...one had to serve. Blow it out? But all she could call up was a puff of air, which seemed to fan the flame instead of extinguishing it. Water? But all she could form was dew, which was not enough to douse the fire. Oh, her feet! Oh, her legs! Cut? Cut! The spell nicked the thongs enough for her to twist her hands and break free of them. She bent, pulled the nightgown around her legs, toppled away from the flames, and rolled on the ground. Sitting up, she saw her clothes had not burned, but her feet, her legs! She spelled a small sphere of light and examined them. Red and blistered only, no black spots, but bad enough. She began to weep from the pain.

"Cry, baby, cry!" mocked Janna.

"Oh, leave the baby to cry," Kelsie said. They walked back to the house.

Painfully, limping on her blistered feet, she made her way to the back door. Elspeth stood inside in the washroom, a lighted lamp on a shelf beside her. "What was all that caterwauling about?"

Marlys hobbled out of the washroom to the main room and pointed to Janna and Kelsie, across the wide space in their own beds. "They tried to kill me!"

"Stop whining at once, or I'll send you home!"

Marlys stood agape.

"Do you want to be a sorcerer?" Elspeth demanded.

Marlys found her voice. "Yes, that's why I came here, but...."

"And you took the oath of an apprentice, saying you would obey me until the high sorcerer determined you were ready to go out in the world as a full sorcerer, no matter what happened."

"Yes, but...."

"Then if you're ever going to do anything but those pitiful household spells, you'll learn not to complain about anything that goes on in my household. Or I'll release you from your oath and send you home. Do you understand?"

She sighed. "Yes, Sorcerer Elspeth."

"Very well, then." Elspeth took the lamp and walked past her.

Marlys limped to her bed and found her sack, which held all the possessions she had. Those included unguents that would help with the burns. A "pitiful household spell" would speed the healing. She settled back into bed, silently weeping into her pillow. She expected her apprenticeship to be hard—everyone told her that being an apprentice, especially to a sorcerer, was hard—but she did not expect it to be brutal. Was this a test, to see if she was resolved? Why had Elspeth, not to mention Janna and Kelsie, who she barely knew, been so cold? In any case, she was not going home. She would show them.

In the days that followed, Marlys found that violence seemed to be the way of the sorcerer. With regularity, Janna and Kelsie attacked Marlys in every way imaginable. They dug a hole, threw her in it, and shoveled dirt on top of her. They threw a sack over her, tied it, and tossed her into a river. Each time, Marlys had to call on all her resources to get free, and only barely survived. If this was teaching, Marlys felt it was bad teaching—why not, rather, show her how to escape such situations first, and after that put her to the test?

With no allies, and Elspeth showing no concern for her suffering, Marlys often thought of going back home. But Marlys knew in her heart that she would never be satisfied with just doing household spells. She wanted to be able to do what she had seen sorcerers do—heal mortal wounds, repel monsters, banish wildfires. But Elspeth never taught her any of that. The only way Marlys learned anything at all was watching and listening on the quiet days when Elspeth spoke to Janna and Kelsie. It seemed she was allowed to do that, because no one protested or prevented her when she did.

Although Marlys tried to follow the lessons Elspeth gave to Janna and Kelsie, nothing happened until one day, while walking near a swamp she had not visited before, she slipped into a clutching bog—so called because the mud closed around the victim, sucking the victim to the bottom. After a moment of panic, Marlys calmed herself. She would not sink all at once. She had time. For now, only her legs had been encased. Reaching for her knife, she jerked it out of the sheath and stabbed the hard ground, trying to pull herself out. But the knife broke. She reached for a nearby young tree, narrow enough so she could grasp it, but she could only brush it with her fingertips. She tried her household magic: reach, bend, stretch. Yes, stretch.

When she cast the spell in her mind, her left leg straightened. She felt a horrible pain as if she had stepped on a long nail. Her leg, from her heel to her knee, stiffened and she threw back her head and gasped in agony. At the same time, her body jerked forward slightly out of the bog.

Slowly, the bog attempted to pull her in again. This time, Marlys concentrated on mentally pushing the sensation of the needle out. With each effort, the needle seemed to move, and her body correspondingly moved out of the mud. But it was too slow, and the bog continued to claim her. Finally, annoyed and desperate, she surged back at the bog with all her might. She popped out, landing hard on her stomach, clear of the mud.

The internal backlash was excruciating. She rolled on the ground, hugging herself. It seemed as if a thousand needles had jabbed through her heels, her palms, her head. She found she could not even cry out, could not breathe. Breathe! There, her lungs filled with air. The pain subsided. She lay there on her back, spent.

After some time, she crawled, then got to her feet, and found she was uninjured. Exhausted, she staggered back to the house.

After that, mostly in bed, at night, while the others slept, Marlys tried to recapture the magic she knew had penetrated her at the bog. She found that she could pull it in and push it out, through her hands, through her feet. The sensation, sharp at first, never felt so agonizing as the first time, and grew less and less painful with practice until it did not hurt at all.

Out of sight of the others, she put the magic into practice. She created wind where there was none. Rabbits came to her against their will. Once, out in the forest, she met a bear. She stopped it in its tracks. Four days later, out hunting, she found the bear still in place. This time, at a safe distance, she released the spell and the bear sauntered away. Finally, one night, when rain beat against the roof, she slipped out the back door to stand in the yard, and not a drop touched her. She raised her arms and her face to the sky in triumph.

One day, she saw Elspeth walk past with Janna and Kelsie.

"Why do you always set us at these mundane tasks?" Kelsie complained. "Make the horses go back to the barn, turn the stream to water the garden...I'd rather cause a wildfire to start and put it out again."

"You have to perfect the small tasks before you can attempt the great ones," Elspeth explained.

"How about the spell where you conjure the image of another sorcerer to talk to her at a distance?" Kelsie suggested.

"That is one of the more powerful spells," Elspeth said. "It is beyond your present ability."

"You might as well ask for the spell for the doorway to the island worlds," Janna told Kelsie.

Elspeth nodded. "That is one of the greatest spells. If you could do that, you would be a sorcerer, not an apprentice."

"I could try it," Kelsie said.

"And if you did?" Elspeth answered. "Unless you were as skilled as I, you would be sucked into that other world, and not come back."

Kelsie said nothing, but caught Janna's eye and smiled, then nodded in Marlys's direction. Marlys guessed that meant that as soon as they were trained, they would certainly try that spell on her.

If Janna and Kelsie planned to open the doorway and push her in, Marlys knew she had to learn to summon it first. One night, when the full moon shone in the back yard, Marlys slipped out. She stood near the barn and faced the spot where the clearing met the woods. Although she had not been given a specific spell to summon the doorway, she had succeeded in previous spells by picturing the result in her mind and drawing the magic in and out of her body. She took a breath, summoned all her strength, stared resolutely in the direction of the woods, and moved her hands as if pushing open a gate.

The maelstrom nearly knocked her down. She had to use magic just to stay in place. Everything near the doorway, however, fell inside, from the fox crossing the yard to the young trees at the edge of the clearing—uprooted and sucked in. Looking ahead of her, she could see what appeared to be a silvery arch, and through it, she spied a moonlit meadow. The gale rushed from behind her into the arch, trying to blow her inside. With a gesture, she closed the door.

All was still. Marlys sunk to the ground and sat there, spent.

The back door opened. Janna and Kelsie rushed out.

"What was that?" Janna shouted.

Elspeth stepped outside. She surveyed the holes in the dirt where the young trees had been, the broken fence around the garden, the grass littered with leaves stripped from the trees.

Kelsie pointed to Marlys. "You idiot! Practicing magic without Elspeth directing you? You could have killed us!"

Elspeth turned to Janna and Kelsie. "Inside!"

With one last withering glance toward Marlys, Janna and Kelsie followed Elspeth to the house.

In the morning, at the breakfast table, Elspeth said simply, "We're going to see High Sorcerer Thorne today."

As Marlys cleaned up, Kelsie leaned toward her and hissed, "You're in trouble now."

Marlys did not much care.

After breakfast, they dressed in their finest and rode to the fortress of the high sorcerer. Elspeth sped them on their way.

When they arrived at the fortress, Marlys saw many other coaches ahead of them. Sorcerers alighted and walked inside. Elspeth, Janna, Kelsie, and Marlys followed.

They walked through a long corridor with a marble floor and arched ceiling. At last, they reached what seemed to be an audience chamber. A long narrow rug led to a throne where the High Sorcerer sat. The other sorcerers stood to either side. They seemed to Marlys to be waiting expectantly.

Elspeth stopped and waved Janna and Kelsie to the walls where the other apprentices lingered. Marlys and Elspeth stood alone before the High Sorcerer.

She stared right at Marlys. "I heard you accomplished something rather remarkable for an apprentice with so little experience."

Marlys said nothing.

"Answer her!" Elspeth whispered in Marlys's ear.

"I may have," she said, looking not at Thorne but the marble floor.

"Do you think to reach the rank of sorcerer so quickly?"

"I wouldn't presume," Marlys said.

Thorne stood. "Come," she said to Marlys.

Marlys followed, aware that Elspeth and the other sorcerers and apprentices strolled behind her. They walked through an arch into a huge enclosed courtyard.

"Let's see how you do with this," Thorne said. With a gesture, she opened the iron gate—which was at least 20 feet tall—to the outside. In stomped a behemoth. It had four legs, each the thickness of tree trunks, and a sinewy neck holding a head with long, cruel teeth. Marlys extended her arm. The creature stopped, bellowed with frustration, and slowly turned and stomped away. Marlys made sure that the behemoth would continue to walk in that direction at least 2 miles. She closed the iron gate behind it from where she stood.

"Very impressive," Thorne said. "Come here, child."

Marlys put her arm down and walked forward. Thorne extended her hand. Warily, Marlys took it. With her other hand, Thorne thrust a knife into Marlys's side.

Marlys doubled over with pain and astonishment. Blood spilled from the wound. After the first moment of panic, she calmed herself and again caused the magic to flow through her and around the knife. Carefully, she drew it out, and the wound closed. She passed the bloody blade to Thorne, who gave it to a sorcerer next to her.

The high sorcerer smiled. "So you are a sorcerer after all."

"Marlys?" shouted Janna and Kelsie, aghast.

"Silence!" Thorne glared at them. She turned back to Marlys. "Welcome to the ranks of your equals."

Marlys then let Thorne hug her, though she did not yield. When the older woman let her go, she said, "Now, swear to me that you will never harm another sorcerer, or your life will be forfeit."

"I swear I will never harm another sorcerer, or my life will be forfeit." Marlys said, and she felt a tingle, realizing that magic had been used to enforce the oath.

"There. The spell is set," Thorne said. "Come, stand beside me at the throne as I formally present you."

Marlys followed her and took a place at Thorne's right hand as the older woman sat. She motioned for the assembly to gather around her. When they were quiet, Thorne said, "Join me in welcoming Sorcerer Marlys."

"Welcome!" "Well done!" the others shouted.

Marlys looked at all of their smiling faces, spread out her hands, and stopped time around them. All froze in their places. Marlys walked through the assembly and outside to the coach, locking all doors and gates behind her. She drove away in the coach she had arrived in, speeded by magic, with a light heart and eager spirit. All of those pitiful sorcerers and apprentices would stay in Thorne's castle until the day she released them, the day that she returned with all of her own apprentices and sorcerers, trained in her way—without malice or cruelty. Which method would convince them then? She would cheerfully wait for that day to come.

Part I: The Revenge Quest

Chapter 1

Having a wedding in a palace full of frozen bodies was not the idea of High Sorcerer Marlys, but that is what the couples asked for, so she consented.

Looking around the otherwise empty audience room, she could appreciate the reason for choosing this location. The palace fortress had exquisite stained glass windows, the walls were of the finest marble, the floor had been set with the finest tile. The ceiling was high, the room was airy. Light of many colors streamed in.

Even the frozen bodies added a decorative touch. Not that they were literally frozen. Marlys had suspended them in time twelve years ago. They remained alive. If she released them, their lives would go on.

For now, they stood as they had for twelve years. Sorcerers all. Dressed in their finery. Tir had adorned them with garlands for the occasion. An outsider might have mistaken them for statues.

The sorcerers and apprentices began streaming in, chatting merrily. Women all, except for Tir. Only a small number of women could generate or use magic, or so it had been thought. Of those women who could use magic, most did not progress beyond household spells. Becoming a sorcerer required training, and talent.

Then came Tir. He was assigned female at birth. He insisted he was a boy as soon as he grew old enough to speak his truth. His family brought him to Marlys and her assembly for his transition. Spells to alter the appearance of a body were well-known and numerous. Transition spells also required changes to the inner workings of the body. None of them had cast a transition spell before, but they consulted their library of spell books, and, after seeing nothing helpful there, made a search of the fortress. Sorcerers in ancient days had simply written spells on parchment and secreted them anywhere that seemed to be a secure hiding place. Eventually, they found the spells they needed placed within walls of the deepest and least visited levels of the fortress, under spell lock which had to be sorcerously broken. As a result, Tir transitioned into the young man he was destined to be. Since he had demonstrated the ability to use household spells, they invited him to come back when he reached the age of apprenticeship. Upon returning, he completed the training and became a sorcerer himself, celebrated by all.

Watching the to-be-married couples, Marlys reflected that marriage, too, had been a change. Sorcerers had been known to be largely uninterested in coupling since ancient times, although, every once in a while, the sorcerous community would hear of a secret dalliance among them. Although unusual, this was not considered scandalous. But after freezing her former colleagues in time, Marlys had discovered that celibacy had been placed upon her—and every other apprentice—by spell without her knowing when she had arrived to be trained. When she had her own apprentices to train, she did not use that spell. As a result, many still chose to remain celibate, as she had, but others had chosen to marry openly. The first marriages were sorcerer to sorcerer, woman to woman. Recently, Marlys had officiated at weddings with women sorcerers and (non-magical) men. None of the sorcerers' ability to use magic, or do their work, had been affected in the least. Marlys could not help but wonder why the celibacy spell had ever been used in the first place. This was one of the questions she had in mind to ask High Sorcerer Thorne if Marlys ever released her from the time-spell.

Everyone at the gathering was younger than Marlys, who became High Sorcerer for the region by default in the absence of Thorne. Once Marlys had frozen her colleagues in time, she was the only sorcerer in the region. Those times had been hard for her. Many tasks required the skills of a sorcerer – binding mortal wounds, repelling intruding behemoths, and everything else a sorcerer was expected to do for her region. She had been forced to find apprentices, and quickly. Marlys had been able to find enough eager young people with the ability and willingness to become sorcerers. But training took time. The apprentices could perform simple household spells, but to do more complex spells needed sorcery.

That was the heart of the matter. High Sorcerer Thorne continued a tradition that had been around for ages and in just about every region, which presumed that in order to progress from performing simple spells to the complex magical tasks of sorcery, cruelty was necessary. Punishment was necessary. Torture was necessary. Marlys had nearly died several times when her fellow apprentices had abused her, supposedly to bring out her sorcerous powers. None of that had worked. Instead, she became a sorcerer, and a powerful one, just from desperately trying to free herself from a clutching bog. The experience had been tremendously painful. But no cruelty had been involved. Once she had demonstrated her skills to High Sorcerer Thorne and the other sorcerers and apprentices on these very grounds, they had accepted her into their ranks as a sorcerer. Afterwards, they had congratulated themselves on making Marlys's training as excruciating as possible, telling her this was lamentable but necessary.

That was all Marlys could take. Having taken a binding oath that she would not harm a fellow sorcerer or apprentice on penalty of death, she could not take revenge and harm them, and she had no desire to do so. Instead, she froze time around the entire group and walked away. Since no one but the spell caster could undo a time-binding spell, she felt secure in the knowledge that they would stay there indefinitely, until she felt it was safe to release them...or until she died.

From time to time, Marlys entertained the idea of releasing them, but every time she saw the joy of her apprentices, the friendships made, the love matches thriving, she could not bring herself to do it.

Tir touched her arm. "Why so solemn? This is a happy occasion."

Marlys turned to him and smiled. "You're right. It's just that every time I'm in this room, it reminds me of what they put me through."

"Haven't you told us that continuing to dwell on those who have wronged us in the past simply gives them power over us?"

"I have. But it is not easy to let it go."

"Not easy, no, but perhaps worthwhile."

Marlys nodded. "I can't disagree with that."

Serena, a slim young woman with a glorious crown of black hair, walked up to them. "Everyone's here. You can start at any time."

"I think I will." Marlys walked up to the steps to the dais where the High Sorcerer's throne stood. The former High Sorcerer stood in front of it, frozen in time, her expression deceptively kind. Marlys, now taller than she, and dressed as elegantly, positioned herself so that she blocked the view of her predecessor.

"Dear friends, we are gathered here in the presence of the Bright Beings and the Ruler of the Universe to bind together our beloved companions Isador and Sorcerer Skye, as well as our fellow Sorcerers Bronwen and Fern. Please come forward."

The two couples approached the dais, standing at the foot of the steps. Isador was a cobbler that Skye had met while performing her sorcerous duties. He wore a princely outfit that Tir had helped him pick out. The sorcerers all wore their finery. Among the gifts the residents of the various regions willingly gave to the sorcerers in exchange for their services, fine clothes were abundant and never lacking.

Marlys opened her mouth to continue the wedding ceremony, but was distracted by a multi-colored circle of spinning light forming at her right. She turned to see two young women step through it.

Before anyone could react, the taller of the two women extended an arm. "You and you and you and you."

The two couples froze.

Instantly, Marlys time-bound the two newcomers. Exclamations of shock and distress from the onlookers met her ears.

"What is it?"

"What's going on?"

"Marlys, what did they do?"

Marlys faced the assembly and raised her voice. "Everyone. Leave. Leave now."

"We aren't leaving you to these scoundrels," Tir said.

"You have to, before they can cast a spell on anyone else. Out of sight will do. Go!" When the others did not move, she added, "I'll tell you what I find. But I cannot find out anything from these two and protect you at the same time."

Rochelle, the most stalwart and strongly-built of the sorcerers, pointed. "That's Zaria."

"Traitor," Serena said.

"Yes, I recognized her, too," Marlys said. "Now go."

"Who's the other one?" Tir asked.

"I'll find out. Go!"

This time the assembly moved out. Marlys was relieved. Most spells, including the most disruptive spells, were line-of-sight spells, that could only be effective if the recipient were within view. The time-binding spell was one of those. Once the other members of the assembly had disappeared around corners, Marlys released Zaria.

"Who's your companion?" Marlys asked.

Zaria glared at her. "Nessa."

"To what do we owe the honor of your presence?"

"You know."

Marlys stifled a sigh. "Pretend I don't."

Zaria held out an arm and swept the room. "We only discussed this a million times."

"Oh, yes, you objected to my keeping these sorcerers frozen in time. So you left. I see you're still an apprentice."

Zaria maintained her icy stare. "I will be a sorcerer one day."

"What?" Marlys scoffed. "Did sewing you into a bag with a couple of angry weasels and throwing you in a river not work?"

"They did not do that."

Marlys grasped Zaria's wrist and extended her arm. "Those bruises and burns show they did something. Recently, too, or else you would have been able to heal them by now."

"None of your affair."

Marlys released Zaria's wrist and turned to Nessa, reversing the time spell.

Nessa came to life. She was younger than Marlys, with straight, light brown hair which brushed her shoulders. Sturdy build, average height. She turned her head from side to side.

"The others are gone. You can't touch them."

Nessa spotted the two almost-wed couples, frozen in place. "I've done enough."

"Yes, you have. I wish to ask you to release them from your spell. They've done nothing to you."

Nessa gestured toward Thorne's still frame. "My aunt did nothing to you."

"That's disputable," Marlys said.

Nessa stepped forward until she stood nearly toe-to-toe with Marlys. She had to look up slightly to make eye contact. "Then let me be clear. Thorne was like a mother to me, after my own mother, her sister, died. She said she'd train me herself to be a sorcerer when I came of age to be an apprentice. She was kind and loving to me. Then you took her away. I've spent the past twelve years becoming a sorcerer, learning spells, building my magical strength, until I could come here and take what you held dear so you could feel the grief that I've felt all these years."

"You've succeeded. First, in becoming a sorcerer. Shortening the distance between two places is an advanced spell, and making a portal end point is something that I can't even do. Second, you have grieved me. Greatly. All of my apprentices, my students who are now sorcerers themselves, and their families are also my family and deeply beloved."

"Good."

"Do not underestimate what I will do to get them back."

"Only I can reverse the spell."

"I know that. Nonetheless."

Nessa took a half step back and faced Thorne. "Release my aunt, and everyone else you have frozen. Then I will release your loved ones."

Marlys regarded Nessa silently for a few moments. "You have no intention of doing so."

Nessa threw back her head and laughed.

"Confirming truthfulness is an advanced spell, but still common. I'm surprised you didn't consider I would use it."

Nessa shook her head. "It doesn't matter. I'll keep your loved ones frozen until eternity passes so that you can suffer as I've suffered."

"That will not bring your aunt back."

Zaria stepped closer. "Or you can die."

Marlys nodded toward Nessa. "She won't kill me. I can tell that when your High Sorcerer confirmed her, she took the same oath as I did. If she harms me, her life is forfeit." Turning back to Zaria, she added, "As for you, you'll find me tremendously difficult to kill."

"What are you going to do, then?" Nessa asked.

"I was just about to ask you that question."

"I learned how to conjure the end portal by studying spells. There are spell books kept by sorcerers for centuries throughout the regions of this world that I have just begun to plumb. I'll find a way to restore my aunt without you. Then you will be left mourning your loved ones for the rest of your life."

"As will everyone else here. Can you afford to make that many enemies? They'll still be here long after I've gone and have memories as along as yours."

"I have little confidence in the powers of a sorcerer who has never known pain."

"In turn, I have scarce confidence in the power of a sorcerer who knows so little about the pain others feel."

Nessa extended her arm and described a circle. The portal reappeared. "We'll see."

"So we shall," Marlys said as Nessa and Zaria walked through the circle and disappeared.

Chapter 2

"They're gone," Marlys called.

Everyone flooded into the room. Sorcerers and apprentices surrounded Isador, Skye, Bronwen, and Fern. Some sobbed. Others touched them. Still others embraced the rigid figures.

Marlys found herself being sought by many who wanted a reassuring hug or a shoulder to hide their faces as they wept. She wished she could hug them all at once. As she did her best to soothe them, her eyes strayed not only to the nearly-married couples, but to the sorcerers she had frozen twelve years ago. She wondered why, in all this time, it had not occurred to her that these sorcerers might have had family that were as grieved about them as she and her sorcerous family were grieving now. As a matter of tradition, many who left their families to train in sorcery seldom saw them again, not for a lack of affection, but simply because most sorcerers isolated themselves for training and work. Apprentices, in particular, were expected to be educated a long distance from where they grew up so that they would not easily give up and go running back to the comforts of home.

Rochelle raised her arms and pointed to the place where Nessa and Zaria had entered. "What are we doing standing around here? We need to go after them!"

Sounds of weeping quieted. Murmurs of assent grew.

All eyes turned to Marlys. "Of course we are going after them. But rushing headlong without thinking will only end in disaster. Fern and Bronwen, and Skye and Isador are safe. They'll remain safe until we can convince Nessa to release them."

"That'll be forever." Celestine, the oldest sorcerer in the room after Marlys, spoke up. "We were children in the same town. She was always stubborn. I went to apprentice here so I didn't have to apprentice with her in the Meadowlands region."

"We could always kill her." Tir's tone did not sound very threatening, however.

Silence greeted his remark.

"No one's killing anyone," Marlys said. "Once we start that, there would be no end to it. Have I taught you nothing about the sorcery wars long past? That's why sorcerers take an oath never to harm each other."

"The apprentices could still act." Before anyone could reply, Tir waved a hand. "I know. I wasn't really serious. The thought did occur, however. And, you never know, she might fall off a cliff due to her own clumsiness."

"Clumsy she is not," Celestine said.

"I wouldn't have any reservations about bringing her here and torturing her a bit," Rochelle said.

Marlys sighed. "We aren't doing that, either. Ending cruelty in sorcery is the reason I froze my former colleagues in the first place."

"She is not going to be easily convinced," Celestine said.

"This is not going to be an easy task," Marlys affirmed. "But that doesn't mean it's going to be impossible."

Serena stepped up, with an open book in her hands. "Knowledge is infinite. There are some spells that we might use to our advantage. The High Sorcerer's fortress in every region has a spell book like ours, recording what they have learned. I've always talked about going through the Spell Passage to learn even more."

"Worth considering," Rochelle said. "Though the spell archives in the fortresses along the Passage are quite a distance away. Traveling to them all would take time."

Serena nodded. "Then there's the legendary Library of Sorcery."

Tir let out a huff. "As if that exists."

Serena appeared undaunted. "It may. My point is, we are thinking that the only way to undo a time spell is for the sorcerer who cast the spell to reverse it. What if there's another way, one lost, or not yet discovered?"

Murmurs of assent filled the silence.

"We need to make a plan," Marlys said. "At the moment, we've all had a shock. Let's take time to rest and gather our thoughts. Perhaps we can discuss this over dinner."

Slowly, in ones, twos, threes, small groups, the assembly dispersed.

* * *

Sorcerers could not conjure food out of nothing. They did receive regular food deliveries from elsewhere in the region in exchange for their services, but they also had a barn with cows and horses, as well as pens for chickens and pigs. Fruit trees grew nearby, and some of the apprentices and sorcerers had planted a vegetable garden. Marlys and Serena, among others, knew how to cook. A number of the apprentices and sorcerers had grown up on farms. As a result, all of them were well-supplied with food.

Since they had anticipated a celebration, a feast had been planned. They served all the food and delicacies that had been prepared, but some found that they had little appetite. Conversation was held in muted tones.

When it seemed that most had eaten their fill, Rochelle spoke up. "What is our plan? Are we making a plan?"

"Yes, we are making a plan," Marlys said.

"Good," Tir said. "What is it?"

Marlys nodded toward Serena. "Serena has cast a locator spell. Nessa is at the High Sorcerer's fortress at Woodlands."

"Collecting allies?" Tir asked.

Marlys turned to him. "Doubtful. This isn't a war. Cases of disputes between sorcerers in different regions are rare, and taking sides in such disputes even rarer."

"Most likely she's studying their spell books," Celestine said.

"That's our guess," Serena said, nodding to Marlys. "She also wants to see if she can remove the time binding without the help of the original spell caster."

"Follow her?" Tir asked.

"Not necessarily," Marlys said. "There are other places we can visit, each with its own unique spell book."

"What if she finds what she wants in the Woodlands and returns here?" Tir asked.

"We'll have someone monitoring the audience room here at all times," Marlys said. "I presume we'll have no lack of volunteers?"

She was answered with several nods.

"If she comes back," Marlys said, "whoever is watching can freeze her in time before she can do anything and hold her until I can come and question her. We can remove her to a safe place while she is stationary if need be."

"Chances are it will take time," Celestine said, "even if such a spell exists."

"Serena and I will go and search for spell books to consult," Marlys said.

Astrid, one of the more recently graduated sorcerers, turned to Marlys. "You're not leaving us?"

"I'm responsible for all of this," Marlys said.

Sounds of protest resounded through the room.

"I am," Marlys said. "If I had not bound my colleagues in time, none of this would have happened."

"Nonsense," Celestine said. "Nessa alone is responsible, and you are not responsible for her actions."

"If you hadn't frozen them, I would not have become a sorcerer," Astrid said. "I would have quit rather than subject myself to cruelty."

Marlys heard sounds of assent. "Nonetheless, I need to be the one to go. A spell to reverse the time binding without the caster may require the strength and experience of a high sorcerer. If we can't find such a spell, I still need to seek Nessa out and somehow try to convince her to reverse the spell." She nodded to Celestine. "Celestine will be in charge in my absence."

"You can't go with just Serena," Tir said. "I'll go, and before you say no, if you leave me behind, I'll just find a way to tag along."

Marlys sighed.

"You need someone with muscle," Rochelle said. "Sorcery can't do everything, and there's no weapon I can't handle."

"We need to be nimble," Marlys said. "That means as few of us need to go as possible."

"Since I'm to be in charge," Celestine said, "I say that four is sufficient. The rest of us will stay here, on watch, and to continue our usual tasks throughout the region. If Serena will leave our spell book, we can use the time to learn more spells and perhaps create new spells."

"New spells take time," Tir said.

Celestine lifted an eyebrow. "If you thought your task would be accomplished in a matter of a few days, Tir, perhaps you'd best remain."

"I'm still going, no matter how long it takes," Tir said.

Apparently feeling the conversation was at an end, many at the table began to push back their chairs and walk out after giving nods and well wishes to Marlys and her company. Soon, only Marlys, Celestine, Tir, Serena, and Rochelle remained.

Celestine turned to Marlys. "I'm not the high sorcerer you are, but I'll do my best in your absence."

"You'll do better than I did when I started out," Marlys said. "I was just stumbling around."

"I think you are too modest," Celestine said. "I remember those days."

"So do I," Marlys said. "There's much that I hid from you and the other first apprentices."

"You hid it well, then," Celestine said.

"And it was not without effort," Marlys said. "After I bound my colleagues in time, I found that I had to take on all the responsibilities of sorcery in the region myself. I was so overwhelmed I actually returned home like a runaway, threw myself in my grandmother's lap, and cried like a baby."

"I remember your grandmother," Tir said. "She was a grandmother to all of us, too."

"Yes, she came back with me to help me."

Rochelle's brow furrowed. "Not with sorcery?"

"No, not with sorcery. But there was so much else I had to learn I didn't even know where to start. When my tears had dried, Grandmother said, 'Now get off my lap, straighten your back, and grow up.'"

Tir laughed. "Dear old granny said that?"

Marlys nodded. "And many other things, though not in your hearing. She said that ordinarily, she'd let me make my own mistakes and learn from them, but since I was now responsible for the region of Goldenvalley, I needed to mature fast, and she would help me."

"Dear old granny," Tir said.

"She was magistrate for the Grasslands region before she retired and my father took over from her," Marlys said. "Her sister was a sorcerer."

"What did she teach you?" Serena said.

Marlys took a deep breath. "If I listed it all, we'd be here all night. But she taught me many things about human nature, how to settle disputes peaceably, how to hold my anger in check, how to handle myself with humility and grace."

"I miss her," Tir said.

"So do I," Marlys said. "Every day. But sorcery can only do so much to extend life, and she made me promise not to try."

"In a sense, she taught me through you," Celestine said.

"Or directly from her," Marlys said. "I know she took a little time to mentor all of my apprentices."

Tir smiled. "But more gently than with you, I'd say."

Marlys nodded.

"I hate to interrupt," Rochelle said, "but when do we leave?"

"As soon as we can pack," Marlys said. "Get a good night's sleep and we can be off some time tomorrow."

Chapter 3

The next day, Marlys, Tir, Rochelle, and Serena gathered in the supplies room with Celestine to put together their carry packs. They were all dressed to travel: sturdy pants, practical shirts, ankle boots.

Each donned a cape of fine purple cloth trimmed with gold piping, marking them as sorcerers. Marlys wore the badge of the region as high sorcerer: a golden tree embroidered against a silver background. Often these identifying garments remained at home, but Marlys felt that if they were to travel outside their region, people ought to know who they were. Friendly neighbors would be more apt to approach them, and highway robbers to avoid them.

Tir glanced at Serena as she packed. "What are you taking?"

"A couple of knives, a cookpot, change of clothes, blood rags, blanket, bedroll, pillow, canteen, plate, cup, utensils...."

Tir's brow furrowed. "No food?"

"We'll get food on the way," Marlys said.

"I"m taking food." Rochelle tied up her pack, then grabbed a saber, crossbow, and some arrows from the wall.

Once everyone seemed ready, Marlys turned to her traveling companions. "This is your last chance to stay. Nessa can locate us with her spells...."

"...and we can locate her," Rochelle said.

Marlys nodded. "...and may time-bind you. She won't do it to me, because she needs me. But she will you."

"She can't take us by surprise again," Serena said. "There are a number of defensive spells I'm ready to use. If I cast them before she can time-bind me, she has no chance."

"I'm ready, too," Tir said.

"Won't get me," Rochelle added.

Marlys turned to Celestine. "Expect her to come back here and try to time-bind anyone she sees."

Celestine nodded to Serena. "As Serena said, she can't take us by surprise again. The apprentices and sorcerers have been meeting and are happily coming up with spells to use against her if she tries."

They all made their way to the main entrance of the palace, where they were met by a crowd of apprentices and sorcerers. Many bid farewell with hugs and waves and good wishes.

Astrid walked toward them, leading a horse drawing a cart.

"I was thinking of walking," Marlys said. "We can use sorcery to shorten the distance."

"I would rather sleep on a cart than on the ground," Tir said.

Serena and Rochelle nodded.

"Very well," Marlys said, placing her pack on the cart. She climbed onto the driver's seat and took the reins from Astrid. Tir sat beside her; Serena and Rochelle sat on the raised seats within the cart.

When they at last were on the road, Tir turned to Marlys. "Where to first?"

"The Meadowlands," Marlys said.

"Nessa and Zaria's region?" Rochelle asked.

"Yes," Marlys said.

"But what would we possibly learn there?" Rochelle asked.

"What Nessa knows," Marlys said.

Even with shortening the distance, Meadowlands was far enough away so that they stopped at the border to rest and water the horse. A river divided Meadowlands from the neighboring province.

Everyone left the cart to stretch their legs while the horse drank. Marlys looked to the other side of the riverbank to see a man point to them. Others joined him.

"I wonder what that's about?" Tir asked.

The man, dressed in a rough shirt and leggings, walked to the river's edge and untied a flat raft. Using a pole, he guided it to the other side. When he reached the shore, he jumped off the boat and bowed slightly.

"Sorcerers?" he asked.

"Yes," Marlys said.

"Thank the Universe," he said. "We've been waiting for one to come for some time. The usual sorcerer who comes has missed her last scheduled visit."

"Who is that?" Marlys asked.

"A sorcerer named Nessa."

Marlys nodded. "I see. How can we help you?"

He pointed to his right. "We've had a lot of problems lately. The bridge is out. We have to use rafts to cross. Our town well is stopped up. We've had to come to the river for water. The millstone at the mill has broken. Farmer Wes had an accident and can't move his legs." He put down his arms and sighed. "It's been difficult for all of us."

Rochelle put a hand on the cart. "I'll take the bridge. We would have had to fix it to take the cart across in any case."

"I'll take the millstone," Serena said.

"I'll take the well," Tir said.

The man turned to him. "A man in sorcery? I've heard of those only in legend."

Tir smiled and laughed merrily. "I am truly legendary, yes."

"I'll come for Farmer Wes," Marlys said. "Just show us the way."

The man poled them across. A group met them at the shore. Residents volunteered to escort the sorcerers to the sites of their tasks. As she walked through the village, escorted by a woman, she noted that the name of the place was Mills Landing.

The woman brought her to a small but sturdy house at the end of a large field of grain. The inside looked well kept. An old woman sat in a rocking chair next to a fireplace.

She looked up at Marlys. "About time we had some return for all the flour we send to the sorcerers."

Marlys's escort murmured, "Hush, granny."

"It's all right," Marlys reassured her. "I had a granny myself."

The woman continued to a room where a man lay in bed. He looked up when they entered.

"The sorcerer is here," the woman said.

Marlys sat in a chair next to the bed.

"You aren't the one we're used to," Wes said.

"No, but I can assure you I'm as skilled as she." Marlys reached out and cast a spell to relieve pain.

"Will it hurt?" Wes asked.

"Not overmuch," Marlys said. "Just be still."

"Will it take long?" the woman asked.

"Not long." Marlys cast the spell, and saw in her mind the broken parts knit, the sinews and nerves reconnect. When the healing was complete, she sat back in the chair and sighed.

Wes reached down. "I can feel my legs again. Thank you."

Marlys nodded and stood. "You can walk right away, though you might be wobbly at first. Try to rest today before starting any work tomorrow."

"He can work tomorrow?" the woman asked.

"Light work for now. He may be sore for a few days, but it will go away."

"Thank you," the woman said.

Marlys stood and smiled. "I'm happy to be of service."

The woman escorted her to the town square. Tir stood next to the well, where villagers already were drawing water.

"Looks like success," Marlys said.

Tir grinned. "Oh, yes. I had quite an audience. The little ones wondered aloud whether I could really do magic. When the water gushed up and filled the basin, they seemed to be amazed."

Marlys smiled. "You are amazing, that's true."

Rochelle walked toward them, leading the horse by the harness. "Bridge is better than ever."

Serena approached from another direction. "Millstone is whole and working already."

"Good work, all," Marlys said. "Let's go on to the High Sorcerer's fortress."

Just as they were about to climb onto the cart, a group of townspeople walked toward them. A young girl carried a basket and stepped forward.

"Sweetcakes," she said, extending the basket. "For your journey."

The four sorcerers stepped up. Each took a cake.

"Mmmm. This is good," Tir said.

Serena nodded after taking a bite. "Yes, very good."

"Best I've had in a while, thank you," Rochelle said.

"Delicious," Marlys added.

A woman standing behind the girl said. "Take the basket, too, with our thanks."

"That's very kind, although you've already shared your goods with the sorcerers in this region." Marlys took the basket.

"Still, a little extra to show our appreciation," the woman said.

* * *

They traveled on until they reached a tall stone edifice.

Tir looked up as they approached. "Sturdy, but not as nice as ours, I think."

"Some prefer practical over pretty," Rochelle said.

They stopped the cart near the entrance and tied the horse to a hitching post. A water trough, about half full, was in reach, as was a bale of hay.

A sorcerer stood in the entrance as they approached. She scanned their capes and spotted Marlys's badge. "Nessa isn't here," she said flatly.

Another sorcerer in finery indicating she was a high sorcerer walked up behind her. "That is not the welcome we give to fellow sorcerers," she chided softly. Turning to Marlys, she added, "High Sorcerer Marlys. It has been some time since we talked through the sorcerous channels."

Marlys inclined her head briefly. "Perhaps too long, High Sorcerer Ilse, though in truth both of us are kept busy with our regional tasks."

Marlys gestured toward her companions. "These are sorcerers from my assembly, Tir, Serena, and Rochelle."

"Come inside," Ilse said.

They followed her through the entrance and walked down wide carpeted corridors. Sorcerers and apprentices they passed glared at them.

One said to Tir as he walked by, "Are you a real sorcerer?"

Everyone stopped.

Tir turned to the speaker. "Yes, I am real. And, yes, I'm a sorcerer."

"What spells can you do?"

Tir held out hand, palm up, and conjured a pillar of light, first in orange and red, then in blue and white.

"I mean a real spell," the speaker insisted.

"Please," Rochelle said. "That's not mere household magic, and you know it."

Tir grinned. "Oh, you mean like this." He reached up, then lowered his hand as if pulling an invisible cord. A lightning bolt crashed outside from a clear sky and shook the building.

The intense light pierced through the windows; the thunder resounded.

Ilse turned to the speaker. "You can tell who another sorcerer is without demonstration, Pix."

Pix bit her lip but said nothing.

Ilse walked on. Marlys and the others followed. Ilse stopped at an open doorway and motioned them inside. The room was small but elegantly furnished. Each took a seat in a richly upholstered chair.

"What brings you here?" Ilse asked. "You already know that Nessa is not here."

"Yes, we stopped at Mills Landing to perform needed services," Marlys said. "Apparently Nessa missed her usual visit."

Ilse sighed. "I told her not to go on her revenge quest. We all did...except Zaria. I thought she'd tell you off and return to her duties in the region."

"She locked three sorcerers and a prospective groom of one of them in a time spell," Marlys said.

"This is the first we've heard of it," Ilse said. "And I am sorry. She shouldn't have done that. But don't mistake me. We don't agree with what you did, either. Releasing High Sorcerer Thorne and her assembly is long overdue. However, that's your affair. We certainly aren't going to fight you over it."

"If it makes any difference," Marlys said, "I'm beginning to see for myself that it's long overdue."

"I assure you, it makes no difference whatsoever," Ilse said.

"But I cannot release them while members of my own assembly are time-bound by her."

"And that," Ilse said, "is the reason we tried to dissuade her. We told her any spells she cast would delay your releasing them, not speed it up."

Tir leaned forward and lifted a finger. "If I may."

Ilse turned toward him.

"How do you elevate your apprentices? The traditional way, or our way?"

Ilse faced him squarely. "There are some here who prefer the traditional way, and we allow it, though less harshly than before. Most apprentices, however, are elevated your way, by having to break through a sorcerous crucible." She turned to

Marlys. "And yes, I admit that it took drastic action to reverse a long-held tradition that a lot of us despised, though we did not say so, and we are truly grateful that it ended. Thorne would not have been convinced by any argument that you, or I, or anyone else for that matter, could have given her. Nonetheless, I did not approve of your methods, and many here agree, as you saw."

"I am not asking you to condone or approve," Marlys said.

"Then why are you here?"

Marlys nodded to Serena. "Serena is the keeper of our spell books. We would like permission for her to read yours."

"I have no objection to that."

"Thank you," Marlys said, and rose from her chair.

Serena also stood. "It will not take long. I have developed a spell that allows me to read quickly."

Everyone was now on their feet. Ilse faced her and raised an eyebrow. "A new spell?"

"We encourage the development of new spells," Marlys said.

Ilse faced her. "So do we, though the efforts are seldom successful."

"We have a large failure rate as well," Marlys said.

"If I may, again," Tir said. "We have a larger measure of success precisely due to our larger rate of failure."

Ilse faced Tir as he spoke but did not reply. Instead, she gestured to the door. "I'll escort you to the spell books."

Chapter 4

After leaving Serena alone with the spell book, Ilse showed them to guest rooms. "Please stay with us overnight. I'll have your meals brought to an adjoining room." She nodded in that direction. "An apprentice will see to your horse."

"Thank you for your hospitality," Marlys said.

Ilse nodded and walked away.

When she was gone, Tir turned to Marlys. "I see we won't be eating in the common room."

"Would you want to?" Rochelle said. "It's plain that they want to see little of us, and I would rather not eat under their glares."

Serena joined them as dinner was being served. The apprentices who brought their food, plates, and utensils said little and left quickly.

Once they were seated, Marlys asked, "What did you find?"

"There are no spells in the book that we do not know," Serena said.

"Good," Rochelle said. "Then they can't take us by surprise by a spell we haven't yet seen from them."

"It is possible," Serena said, "that she knows spells not in the book, like that end-point spell of hers, which she said she discovered somewhere, but my guess is that she doesn't know any unique spells beyond that."

"The same spells have been handed down for centuries in every region," Marlys said. "New spells are rare. She probably took years researching that spell of her own."

"The unwritten spells passed from sorcerer to sorcerer tend to be weak ones," Serena said. "At least, that's what I've experienced."

"Where do we go next?" Rochelle asked.

"Woodlands," Marlys said, "to see what Nessa found there."

"Are we just going to follow her?" Rochelle said.

"Not necessarily," Marlys said. "We have to track Nessa. We must. As with any sorcerer, she could do great harm. While we are doing that, however, we need to collect clues that will point us to the Library of Sorcery."

"Do you think it exists?" Rochelle said.

"It may or may not," Marlys said. "If it does exist, we need to find it."

"Before Nessa does," Tir said.

"Before Nessa does," Marlys affirmed. "And, such a library could have the knowledge of many beneficial spells."

"Or many harmful ones," Rochelle said.

"Any spell can be beneficial or harmful," Tir said, "depending on how it is used."

"On my journey from my birthplace in Majesticacres," Serena said, "I stopped at sorcerer training centers in every region between here and there. At every place I tarried, every place, sorcerers mentioned the Library. Either it is a popular myth, or it is a real place."

"Perhaps a little of each," Tir said. "A real place, but exaggerated as tales grew through the years."

"Maybe a small lodge with only a shelf of spell books," Rochelle said.

"I've retained all the information I could," Serena said. "And have tried to gather more, but the bits of knowledge of it are very scarce. Most tales agree that the Library is in or near the Shadowmount."

Rochelle groaned. "The highest mountain among the Mountains of Wrath. Guarded by its own spells. Bane of sorcerers."

"You have to admit," Tir said, "if you want to establish a secret library where no one will want to touch it, that's the place to build it."

"It may be less than its reputation," Marlys said.

"Or more," Rochelle said.

Marlys nodded. "Whichever it is, we need to try to find it."

The next day, they left quietly, without a farewell from anyone. The horse had been tended to and had been left alone hitched to the cart, tied to the post near the fortress entrance.

At midday, they stopped to rest and water the horse and eat a meal. They had received extra food at breakfast with the silent understanding that they could bring the leftovers with them. Marlys passed out plates and they settled on the seats in the cart to eat.

They were just cleaning up the crumbs when they saw a circle of light form near them.

"Scatter!" Marlys said.

Tir ran behind a tree with a thick trunk. Serena knelt behind a collection of boulders. Rochelle crouched behind tall bushes.

Marlys climbed out of the cart and stood in front of the circle. As she expected, Nessa and Zaria stepped through.

"To what do we owe the pleasure?" Marlys asked.

Nessa scowled. "You went to Meadowlands."

"Yes, we did. What of it?"

"You were poisoning them against me!"

"Against us," Zaria added.

Marlys's brow furrowed. "Did you go there, or simply trace us with a locator spell?"

"I didn't have to go there to know what you were doing!"

"Perhaps you ought to speak with High Sorcerer Ilse. She'll tell you what I said." Marlys turned to Zaria. "And that I mentioned nothing of you at all."

"Why else would you go there?" Nessa said.

"To read their spell books. Sorcerers do that," Marlys said blandly. "You must know that sorcerers visit each other from time to time to exchange knowledge?"

"I have trouble believing that's all you did," Nessa grumbled.

"Believe what you wish," Marlys said. "I've told you the truth. Use a truth spell if you don't believe me."

Nessa stared at Marlys for a moment but said nothing.

Zaria looked around. "Where are the others?"

"Watching you and ready to act if you try to use sorcery against us," Tir called.

A crossbow bolt flew past Nessa's ear.

"Watch that!" Nessa called. "You nearly hit me."

"I shot to miss," Rochelle called.

"I see you two have changed your hair," Tir called. "Shorter hair looks nice on you."

"As if you didn't know," Nessa said.

"No, we don't know," Marlys said.

"Do you think we would believe you haven't used sorcerous channels to talk to your friends at Goldenvalley?" Zaria said.

Marlys spread her hands. "I say again, you can believe what you wish, but we haven't spoken to anyone from Goldenvalley since we left."

Nessa looked directly at Marlys again. "It's the truth." She let out a breath. "We paid another visit to your fortress. We thought for certain that you would go there after you went to Meadowlands. We wanted see if you would relent now that you have had time to think it over."

"Your assembly froze us in time the instant we stepped out of the circle," Zaria said.

"When we came to our senses," Nessa said. "We were lying in a meadow."

"They removed every hair on our heads!" Zaria protested.

Rochelle laughed.

"I see you didn't lack the sorcery to grow it back." Marlys looked at Nessa. "Somewhat, anyway."

Nessa glared at her. "I found you to tell you we aren't going back there if we're going to be ambushed."

"Good. That was the idea," Marlys said. "And if I may say so, if you had used a locator spell instead of presuming I had returned there, you would have avoided being ambushed in the first place."

Nessa frowned. "Don't count on my asking you again. When you're ready to release the time-bind on my aunt and the others, you'll have to find me."

Marlys nodded. "I understand." She motioned behind her. "I hope we've made the point that you'll be stopped again if you try any noxious spells on me or my traveling companions."

Nessa looked around.

Marlys saw that Serena, Tir, and Rochelle remained out of view to avoid Nessa casting a nasty spell on them.

Nessa moved closer until she stood nearly toe-to-toe with Marlys. "Let me make myself plain. I may have had some setbacks, but I intend to keep on hurting you and yours until you feel so beaten that you'll release your time spell."

"Why not just release yours? I give my oath that I will then release my time spell and we can both go on living our lives."

"You haven't suffered nearly as much as I have. I am going to balance the scales."

"You have no idea how much I have suffered in my life."

"Not enough, apparently."

"Appearances are not facts." When Nessa did not respond immediately, Marlys added. "At least concentrate your efforts on me. I'm the one who originated the time-spell on your aunt and the others."

"Our experience at the Goldenvalley fortress and just now tells me that your friends are equally complicit in your crimes and equally willing to move against me."

"When you time-bound our friends, you hurt us as well," Rochelle called from her hiding place.

"This is not over." Nessa conjured the glowing circle.

Before Nessa and Zaria could step through, Marlys called, "When you're ready to relent and release the time-bind on my friends, find me. My proposal holds."

Nessa paused, lowered her head, and stepped through the circle. Zaria followed. The circle disappeared.

The others came out from their hiding places.

"They're still determined," Tir said.

Marlys took a deep breath. "They are. I would hope that they would tire of their quest for revenge, but I know all too well there are those who can hold on to a grudge for years, if not lifelong."

"Let's hope that Nessa and Zaria aren't among them," Tir said.

"That's the reason we need to find our own solutions, in case they never give up," Serena said.

The Woodlands fortress appeared delicate and palatial, but Marlys knew that the walls were as sturdy as the ones in Goldenvalley.

"Nice design," Tir said. "I like the spires."

"The grounds are well kept, too," Rochelle said. "Someone with an artistic eye must have planted everything."

A group of sorcerers strolled out of the entrance as they approached. Marlys signaled the horse to stop, handed Serena the reins, and climbed of the cart. She walked up to meet them.

When everyone was within hearing range, they all stopped.

"Do you come in peace?" High Sorcerer Ware said.

"We do," Marlys said. "All we ask is to read your spell book."

"We wish to be clear that we are not listening to any disputes that are not our business," Ware said.

"We will respect your wishes," Marlys said.

Ware nodded and smiled. "Then as fellow sorcerers, you are welcome." She motioned for an apprentice to take the horse and cart, then led Marlys and the others inside.

They waited in a comfortable room as Serena went to read their spell book. An apprentice brought refreshments. Ware and Marlys sat in high-backed, richly-upholstered chairs across from each other.

"My companions and I have been discussing the legend of the Library of Sorcery," Marlys said.

Ware nodded. "That is also an interest of mine, as well as other sorcerers in my assembly."

"What can you tell us?"

"I wish I could tell you more than you probably know already," Ware said. "Before I became high sorcerer here, I made the attempt to find it myself."

"You've seen the Mountains of Wrath?" Tir said eagerly. "What were they like?"

Ware turned to him. "As formidable as the legends say. Just to stand near the foothills gives one a feeling of dread. There seems to be no place to put a hand, or a foot, or a rope. Simply making the attempt to walk forward is a strain on the body." Ware motioned to one of the other sorcerers. "Junia, here, made the attempt as an apprentice, and simply straining against the Shadowmount's spells allowed her to awaken her sorcery."

Junia leaned forward in her chair. "I would not recommend that as a method, however. I nearly died and was spent for days afterward."

"I made the attempt as an apprentice," another sorcerer said. "And did not even return as a sorcerer. It is not a reliable method to awaken sorcery."

Ware turned to Marlys. "There is something there. Something sorcerous. I could sense it."

"Anyone going there can sense it," Junia said.

"Most turn back well before they reach the foothills," Ware said. "The only few determined souls I know who have even reached that far are in this room."

Junia nodded. "I thought I saw a structure, as if a castle had been carved in the side of the Shadowmount. But as soon as I thought I spied it, it faded. I still don't know whether it was merely a trick of the light or whether something actually there knew I had seen it and hid itself."

Ware spread her hands. "I wish I could tell you more, but that's all we know."

Marlys nodded. "That's a good deal more than any of us knew this morning. Thank you."

Chapter 5

Ware offered them rooms for the night and invited them to join the others later in the common room for dinner. An apprentice brought their packs to the sleeping rooms, which had a lounge where Marlys and her companions settled in.

"Serena is long in coming," Rochelle said.

"Maybe they have an exceptionally thick book," Tir said.

"She'll come when she can," Marlys said, "Perhaps there was a particular spell she wanted to study."

At that moment, Serena appeared in the open doorway. She walked in and sat in an empty chair.

"Find anything interesting?" Tir asked.

Serena sighed. "No, Nessa would not have learned anything here that we didn't know already."

"I wonder if she was here or was shooed away, from the reception Ware gave us," Rochelle said.

"Oh, she was here," Serena said.

"How do you know?" Tir asked.

"An apprentice came in while I was studying the books. She watched me until I finished, then asked if I was from the Majesticacres region."

"And when you told her you were?" Marlys said.

"She asked if I would braid her hair. She said no one here could braid her hair in that style. I did, and while I was braiding, she said a great many interesting things."

"I wonder why she didn't go to Silvervale," Tir said. "They braid hair in the Majesticacres style."

"I'm coming to that," Serena said companionably.

"Yes! A story! Tell us!" Tir said.

Serena settled into a chair. "There are two stories to tell, hers and Nessa's."

"Oh, good, I wondered what Nessa was up to here," Rochelle said.

"Yes," Marlys said, "since we pledged to Ware not to bring it up, someone else would have had to tell us."

"Leticia was more than forthcoming," Serena said. "I didn't even have to ask. She just launched into it. It seems that Nessa and Zaria arrived at the doorstep here and asked to see Ware. Of course, the sorcerers here, not knowing why, just assumed it was a routine matter and brought her to Ware."

"What did Ware say to her?" Marlys asked.

"Nessa asked if there was anything in the spell books to reverse a time-bind without the action of the time-binder. Ware told her no, of course you know you can't reverse such a spell absent the caster. Ware wanted to know why she asked. Was there an emergency? Did something happen in Meadowlands she should know about?"

"And when Nessa told her?" Rochelle prompted.

Serena smiled. "Ware told her, in essence, to go away, she was not getting in the middle of any disputes, especially an old one that had existed for years."

"Did she go?" Tir asked.

"A group of the sorcerers here had to escort her out, but yes, she went," Serena said.

"And Leticia's story?" Marlys said.

Serena took a breath. "Very similar to mine."

"I hadn't heard of yours," Tir said. "You became a sorcerer before I even arrived in Goldenvalley."

"A lot of my experience growing up was common to all of us," Serena said. "I found out I could use household magic and wanted to be a sorcerer. My family, however, was against it. They said I was a fragile, delicate child, and though the training methods of sorcerers was a closely kept secret...."

"And we know the reason for that now," Rochelle grumbled.

Serena nodded. "...they did know that the training was hard and felt I wouldn't survive it. I knew better, and when I reached the age where young people seek apprenticeships, I sought out all the training centers in the region. They all said the same as my family: I was too delicate and fragile. After I had visited all the training centers in my region, I started to go to the other regions. Again, too delicate and fragile, they said. I knocked on training center door after training center door for a couple of years. They'd invite me to stay overnight, or for a week, or a month, as a guest. I'd accept their invitation hoping that once they saw me, got to know me, that they'd realize I could be a sorcerer, but no."

"That's harsh," Tir said.

"How did you support yourself all that time?" Rochelle asked.

"I knew how to live off the land," Serena said. "Finding fruits, vegetables, small birds, rabbits, that was easy with my household magic. Besides, I also know how to sew. A town of any size would have a clothing shop where I could find work for at least a brief time. The training centers were happy to have me sew or cook for them while I was under their roofs, but not as an apprentice."

"I'm sorry that you had to deal with that," Tir said.

Serena nodded at Marlys. "Then I found Marlys."

Marlys smiled.

"When I said I wanted to be a sorcerer, she asked if I would take off my socks and boots so she could see my feet."

Tir turned to Marlys. "Her feet?"

"Yes, I told that Serena if she walked all the way from Majesticacres by herself, and knew enough household magic to keep her feet free of callouses and blisters, she was tough enough to be a sorcerer."

"I was overjoyed," Serena said. "Of course I was proud to show that my feet were in prime condition."

"And Leticia also walked all the way here from Majesticacres?" Tir asked.

"Yes," Serena said, "but in her case, they said she was too awkward and clumsy. Every training center she stopped at didn't even let her ask if she could be a sorcerer. They simply saw that she was unsteady in gait and grasp and turned her away."

"That's sad," Tir said.

"It is," Serena said. "When she arrived here, however, High Sorcerer Ware simply asked her the reason for her visit. When Leticia said she wanted to be a sorcerer, Ware said, like Marlys said to me, that if she had walked this far with only household magic, there was no reason for her not to be a sorcerer."

"If she had come to me, I would have told her the same," Marlys said.

Rochelle turned to Serena. "But then, why not go to Silvervale to get her hair braided?"

"She's an apprentice and can't shorten the distance herself. She'd have to ask one of the sorcerers to bring her."

"The sorcerers here all seem kind," Rochelle said. "I think they'd take her if she'd just ask."

Serena said, "When you've been turned away as much as I have, or as Leticia has, you're reluctant to ask for any favors, thinking that you barely got in and others might use any excuse to ask you to leave. I know I was afraid, for a time, to ask any favors of Marlys. Not now, of course, but then...."

"I'll drop a hint to Ware before we leave," Marlys said. "Surely there's some business in Silvervale that she'd have to send a sorcerer and apprentice to."

"The limitations of sorcery," Serena said. "We can make hair grow, we can remove hair, but we can't cut, style, or braid it with magic. Universe knows how many have tried."

"If sorcery could do everything, would life be worth living at all?" Marlys said.

"A question for philosophers," Tir said. "I'm happy to be a sorcerer and leave questions such as that to others."

Serena turned to Marlys. "I located Nessa before leaving the spell room. She has gone to one of the abandoned training centers in the north of Goldenvalley."

Marlys nodded. "We located her, too. I spoke to Celestine over the sorcerous channels to tell her what Nessa said to us. They're remaining alert."

Rochelle turned to Marlys. "Isn't it time to populate the abandoned training centers? After time-binding Thorne and her assembly, there were too few of us to scatter throughout the region, but there seem to be enough of us now."

"You may have noted," Marlys said, "that as we have had couples get married, I've been assigning them to the abandoned centers. In fact, I had in mind for Bronwen and Fern, and perhaps Skye and Isador as well, to occupy that training center."

"All the more reason to find some other way to release the time-binding spell as soon as we can," Tir said.

"Should we still try to find the Library of Sorcery?" Serena asked.

"We were discussing that with Ware and her assembly while you were reading the spell books," Marlys said. "We'll tell you all we learned later."

Tir leaned in Serena's direction. "To summarize, it's an even a more daunting task than rumors have led us to believe."

Serena nodded.

"Where do we go next, then?" Rochelle asked.

"We'll have to keep Nessa and Zaria as close as safety will allow," Marlys said. "If we get too far away, and they create a disaster, we don't reach them in time even with the distance-shortening spell."

Rochelle took a deep breath and let it out. "Marlys, I respect your experience and your authority, but Nessa is determined not to give up, and won't be convinced to relent anytime soon, if ever. Eventually, we will have to leave her to her own devices and try to find the Library ourselves."

"And Nessa will eventually come to the same conclusion: that if we won't be convinced to relent no matter what she does, she will have to go to find the Library. When she starts to seek it out, that's when we go there."

"I would hope we would find a way to get there ahead of her," Serena said.

"That is how I plan to spend our efforts," Marlys said.

"I like that plan," Tir said.

"In the meantime, where do we go?" Rochelle said.

"The foothills of the Looming Mountains close by have many hideouts we can use that Nessa won't know about," Marlys said.

"I didn't know there were any," Tir said. "That's behemoth country."

"That's how I found the hideouts," Marlys said. "You see, Thorne liked to keep a behemoth or two close by to test sorcerers. She used one to test me. One of the first things I did once she was time bound was to drive the behemoths back into the mountains. It's their natural habitat. I'm sure they were happy to be back home where they could feast on their traditional fare of fellwolves and gigantuans instead of on sheep, goats, cows, and occasional humans."

"Thorne used behemoths to test sorcerers?" Tir said. "I'm doubly happy you time-bound her, then."

"Are the hideouts abandoned behemoth caves?" Serena asked.

"No, they're small stone shelters tucked away in the foothills," Marlys said. "They have acted as way stations for people passing through or recluses who want to be alone. There's an understanding that you can use any shelter that's unoccupied."

"I presume they're empty most of the time," Rochelle said.

"Yes," Marlys said. "I saw no one else when I was corralling behemoths."

"If we didn't know about them, I doubt Nessa does," Rochelle said.

"That is my guess," Marlys said.

They set off the next day, made a stop at midday, and by evening reached the foothills of the Looming Mountains. Marlys guided the horse along narrow roads until they reached a pile of rocks at the foot of a tall rise.

Marlys reined in the horse. "We're here."

"Where?" Tir said.

Marlys climbed down from the cart seat and stood in front of the rockslide. She gestured. Small rocks, pebbles, and dust flew away, revealing a door.

"Now that," Tir said, "is well hidden."

Marlys turned to him. "The house is well built of stone, but over the years, small rockslides have buried it so that it's nearly impossible to find if you don't know where it is."

Rochelle tended to the horse and cart while the others went inside. Tir kindled a sorcerous light. The structure had only one room, with cots, a table and chairs, a counter, and a hearth to build a fire.

"Is there a flue?" Serena asked, examining the hearth.

Marlys gestured. They heard a small rumble. "There is. I've just cleared it."

After they settled in, Serena used a locator spell. "Nessa hasn't moved."

"Good," Marlys said. "We can just keep watch."

They made a supper and ate at the table. After they finished, Marlys said, "Let's go outside. I can show you some of my work."

They climbed the hill, which afforded an excellent view of the Looming Mountains above, and the valley below, which was golden with the grain the region was named for.

Tir pointed. "Is that a behemoth over there?"

They all turned in that direction. Behemoths had four legs, each the thickness of tree trunks, and a sinewy neck with long, cruel teeth and sharp, thick claws. Because they usually walked upright on their hind legs, they were easily spotted, even at a distance.

"It is," Marlys said. She pointed to the southeast. "See that space between the ridges over there? I blocked it with a landslide so that the behemoths were penned in. I did the same all along the foothills here."

"Must have been quite a task," Rochelle said.

"It was," Marlys said. "But worth it. There hasn't been a behemoth coming into the valley since."

In the evening, they all settled into the cots for a good night's sleep.

Just after sunrise, a loud rumbling awakened them.

Tir sat up. "What is it? Avalanche?"

"I'll check," Marlys said. "You stay here." She rushed out and climbed until she reached the top of the hill. Looking out, she saw that the rocks blocking the space had slid down into the foothills, creating an opening.

Below, Serena rushed out from the shelter. "Nessa has moved. She's just beyond the ridge to the east." Serena pointed.

Marlys called to her. "She's releasing the behemoths."

Chapter 6

Knowing the opening must be closed to stop the behemoths, Marlys immediately cast a spell to cause a blocking rockslide. She was not surprised when her work was countered by a spell to open the fissure again. Marlys could not see Nessa, but knew it had to be her acting in opposition. Casting a second spell, Marlys caused a second landslide to seal the gap that Nessa had opened.

Rochelle and Tir walked out of the shelter, just as Marlys closed another fissure. Nessa had not yet attempted to clear the barrier Marlys had just created.

"What's going on?" Tir asked.

"Nessa is trying to open the rockslide walls keeping the behemoths in," Marlys said.

"What can we do?" Tir asked.

"Remember the other blockages I showed you last night?" Marlys said. "She'll go after them next. Tir, take the ones to the east. When she removes them, restore them. Serena, the same, only take the ones nearest us."

"I'll go after Nessa herself," Rochelle said.

"You're pledged not to harm her," Tir said, "What can you do?"

"Distraction, and I have no such obligation to Zaria," Rochelle said.

"Go ahead," Marlys said.

The three sorcerers disappeared, not from invisibility, but because they had shortened the distance between them and their destinations. This action quickly moved them out of sight.

Marlys stayed on watch. She had an unimpeded view of a vast area from her vantage point. As she had feared, the rumblings from all the rockslides attracted behemoths like a dinner bell. Gigantuans, enormous dark footless blobs which could pass over any terrain on their rippling belly muscles, came out of hiding. Although they posed no danger to animal life, their appetite for plants threatened the crops in the valley below. At least she had not seen any fellwolves. Yet.

Having done all she could at a distance, Marlys spelled herself closer to Nessa and Zaria. They stood in a clearing between the foothills and the woods just north of the grain fields. Nessa alternated between pivoting toward the foothills, creating fissures for the behemoths to stomp through, and pivoting toward Marlys's companions, pushing them back. Marlys saw Tir near a clump of sweetbushes, bleeding. Rochelle sat a short distance away, her back against a large rock.

Zaria pointed to Marlys. "And there's Marlys!"

Before Nessa could fully turn in her direction, Marlys pushed against them with sorcerous strength. Nessa and Zaria slid backwards on their feet as if pounded by a mighty wind. Mindful not to cause injury, she pushed them into a distant thicket.

Rochelle raised a hand signaling she was in no immediate danger before pointing to Tir.

Marlys rushed to Tir. His clothes had been cut through and he was bleeding badly. It looked as if he had been raked by large, sharp claws.

"Behemoth," he groaned.

Marlys nodded. "Stay still. The wounds are too deep for you to heal quickly by yourself."

He nodded. "It's been all I can do to conjure the spell against pain."

As she worked, she said, "Where's Serena?"

"She went after the fellwolves Nessa pulled in from the hills."

"What about Rochelle?"

"She freed me from the behemoth that came up behind me while I was blocking another. The behemoth slammed her against the rocks." He turned his head. "Uh-oh. Nessa and Zaria are advancing again."

Marlys glanced in their direction. They remained a fair distance away but would become a threat before she could finish healing Tir. At the same time, she caught a glimpse of an advancing gigantuan. The beast, about four feet in diameter and a couple of feet thick, was unmistakable.

She pulled off a branch from a sweetberry bush and handed it to Tir.

"This has enough berries on it to attract its attention. If we can get it between Nessa and us, it could buy us some time."

Tir waved the branch. "Here, gigantuan. Here, boy. Come get some sweetberries. You know you like them. Yes, you do."

The gigantuan's eyes, protruding from short cylindrical stalks at either side of its head, focused in their direction. Marlys heard an enthusiastic huff and a loud sniff.

Meanwhile, Nessa and Zaria, who undoubtedly knew full well a gigantuan would not attack them, made straight for Marlys and Tir.

Tir continued to croon to the gigantuan, who bounded toward them with amazing speed. It collided with Nessa and Zaria, knocking them to the ground.

Once it reached Marlys and Tir, Tir fed the creature the branch. It remained still, happily munching. Once the branch had been consumed, the gigantuan moved forward a little more to eat from the sweetberry bushes.

Marlys completed her healing task. Tir would be weak for the next day or so, but he was whole.

The gigantuan moved to the side. Marlys heard Nessa say, "Ugh. Get this beast off me."

"Get him off yourself," Marlys said. "You're a sorcerer."

Nessa pushed the creature aside. The gigantuan seemingly accepted the slight change in position as it continued feasting.

Marlys helped Tir to his feet.

Nessa, meanwhile, turned her gaze northward and removed another barrier, releasing even more behemoths.

"Aren't you ready to give up yet?" Tir said.

"Never."

As the gigantuan moved on in its foraging, Marlys saw Zaria sprawled on the ground. Her eyes were closed, and her temple was bleeding.

"Nessa, you need to tend to Zaria," Marlys said. "She's hit her head on a rock."

Nessa glanced at Zaria. "She'll be fine. Stop trying to distract me."

"No, I'm not trying to distract you, and no, she will not be fine," Marlys said. "Head wounds have to be tended as soon as possible or there can be lasting damage that even sorcery can't heal."

Nessa redoubled her efforts to get more behemoths into the area. "You're the one to blame. You lured the gigantuan."

"It's not about blame," Marlys said. "It's about being responsible to those who are in your care."

"She'll be fine, and I can heal her after I'm finished with you."

Tir turned to Marlys. "Heal Zaria. I don't have my full strength back, but I can keep us safe for now."

Marlys knelt beside Zaria.

"Turn your heads," Tir said.

"I'm not taking instructions from you," Nessa snapped.

"I wasn't talking to you." Tir covered his eyes with a hand and produced a blinding flash. The behemoths paused for a moment and changed from walking on their hind legs to advancing slowly on all four limbs.

"Did you think I would find a bright light a hindrance?" Nessa said.

"That wasn't for you," Tir said.

The gigantuan, who had been facing away from the flash, had finished devouring the bushes. It turned in Nessa's direction, and again knocked her over in pursuit of other food.

"Didn't recover from the flash fast enough to see the gigantuan coming, I take it," Tir said.

Over by the rocks, Rochelle had struggled to her feet. "I've healed my cracked ribs and am getting my breath back."

Meanwhile, the behemoths, recovering from the sudden bright light, were on their feet again. One went straight for Nessa.

"Nessa," Tir warned, "you're about to get slashed."

Nessa had her left arm extended to turn a behemoth around and toward Rochelle. To address the danger on her other side, Nessa extended her right arm to repel the advancing behemoth, while another behemoth stalked around and behind her.

Marlys had been glancing up now and then to be sure none of the beasts had come too near. She was about to push at the nearest behemoth when Tir used sorcery to throw rocks at the behemoth's face. The beast stopped and put its front paws to its head.

Zaria stirred. Finished with her healing task, Marlys helped her up.

Nessa sidled over, left arm still extended toward Rochelle, and grasped Zaria's arm. "I've given them enough to cause them grief for now. Let's go." She made a circular motion with her right arm.

"You might have noticed that we saved you both from serious harm, if not death," Rochelle called out.

As the glowing circle formed, Nessa called back. "I don't care. Your gestures mean nothing as long as my aunt and the others are still time bound." She stepped through with Zaria and the ring closed behind them.

Marlys helped Tir to his feet and strode toward Rochelle. The behemoths now turned their full attention to the sorcerers. "If we stand back to back in a triangle, and just fend them off, eventually they'll get tired and hungry and move away."

"If we don't get weary and hungry first," Tir said.

They had little time left for talking, since the behemoths angrily closed in. Marlys did her best to make up for Tir's and Rochelle's depleted conditions, though both of the younger sorcerers cleverly used weaker spells to keep the behemoths out of reach. Tir could not bring down a bolt of lightning, but he could produce a lightning sprite to shock and startle the behemoths. Between spells, Rochelle put her fighting skills to good use, striking toes and knees and other behemoth soft spots.

Suddenly, the ground shook, rocking both sorcerers and behemoths off balance.

"Earthquake?" Tir asked.

Sorcerers came into view: sorcerers from Goldenvalley, Celestine and Astrid in the lead.

"I worked very hard on that spell. I'm glad it worked," Celestine said.

The sorcerers from home gathered around Marlys, Tir, and Rochelle. Working as a team, they repelled and corralled the behemoths.

When the behemoths had been driven a comfortable distance away, Celestine rushed up and hugged Marlys, then Tir, then Rochelle. "Sorry we're late. I was monitoring Nessa's location when Serena connected with us through the sorcerous channels and said you needed help. Even though we shortened the distances, the journey still took time."

Marlys smiled and sighed. "I'm just glad you're here. Where's Serena?"

Celestine pointed. "Over there. She reached us through the sorcerous channels between pushing back fellwolves."

Marlys nodded. "Good work on Serena's part. I would have opened a sorcerous channel myself, but we were overwhelmed."

"I don't doubt it," Celestine said.

Serena spotted them and ran over. "Are you...?" She stopped and stared at Tir's torn and bloody clothes. "Tir!"

Tir smiled. "Healed! No need to worry."

Serena let out a breath. "Seems as if you had the worst of it."

Marlys reached out and put a hand on Serena's shoulder. "You dealt with fellwolves and opened the sorcerous channels. That is no small task."

Celestine looked around. "Nessa and Zaria are gone? Shall we cast a locator spell now or wait?"

"They'll need some time to recover themselves," Marlys said.

Rochelle gestured toward Marlys. "Marlys healed Zaria from a head injury...."

"...after expending herself to heal me," Tir added.

"...and after Nessa refused, and Marlys received not as much as a thank you," Rochelle continued. "Ingrate."

"If I were Zaria, I wouldn't have gone back with Nessa after that," Serena said.

"She doesn't know Nessa refused," Marlys said. "Zaria was unconscious when that happened."

"I wonder what explanation Nessa will give her," Tir said.

"Probably none," Marlys said.

"Speaking of Nessa," Rochelle said. "We kept her from being mauled by a behemoth and received no gratitude for that, either. Only scorn."

Astrid approached the group. "Serena pushed all the fellwolves Nessa released back over the barrier. What do we do with the behemoths?"

Celestine sniffed the air. "They are rather pungent, and all the more so in a pack."

Marlys nodded. "I can give instructions as to where to put them and how to close the gaps so they won't bother us again. I did it before after I time-bound Thorne."

Celestine raised an eyebrow. "All by yourself?"

Marlys took a deep breath. "It took weeks and it was exhausting. But they've kept to the Looming Mountains ever since."

"I'm impressed," Astrid said. "I have an even higher estimation of your powers than before, and my esteem was high already."

"Don't elevate me too high," Marlys said. "I make mistakes and fail as much as anyone else."

After Marlys pointed out where and how to close the gaps in the rock walls, the sorcerers set out to herd the behemoths back to their traditional homes.

"Oh, and there's a gigantuan out there, too," Tir said. "He can't eat the grain all at once, but we need to lead him home, too."

"I'll go after him if you point the way," Astrid said.

Tir pointed. "We last saw him going that way. Be gentle, he helped us out."

"I will." Astrid walked away.

Celestine turned to Marlys. "Nessa has to be restrained. If we hadn't assembled here, those beasts could have done real damage to the region."

"I agree," Marlys said, "but that brings up the age-old question: how to restrain a fully-trained sorcerer? Criminal sorcerers have been banished to the island worlds, but we need her to release our friends, so we can't do that. There's no prison we can fashion that will hold a sorcerer. She's bound by her sorcerer's oath not to harm another sorcerer, but you know that she won't consent to be bound by any other oath while on her quest for revenge. The only way to restrain her would be to time-bind her, but that won't help us, either. She'd have to be released eventually, as stubborn as ever."

"Then that, too, is something we need to bend our minds to, in addition to finding another way to release a time-binding spell," Celestine said.

"You and the other sorcerers can continue to come up with a spell for that and any other spell that might help us," Marlys said. "If you do, you can always reach me through the sorcerous channels."

"Aren't you coming back with us?" Celestine asked. "For rest, at least."

Marlys shook her head. "If I were to go back, the temptation would be to stay. The farewells would be harder. No, I need to stay in motion."

"As will I," Tir said.

"I'm staying with Marlys," Serena said.

"I've made my choice," Rochelle said.

Celestine nodded. "I understand. The blessings of the Bright Beings go with you."

Chapter 7

Marlys and her companions returned to the stone shelter. Rochelle fetched water from the well outside. Serena started supper. Tir changed his clothes. Sorcery was not much use in mending fabric. Household spells could make minor fixes on cloth but could not repair the substantial rips and tears on Tir's shirt.

Marlys cast a locator spell. "Nessa's back at the Meadowlands fortress."

"What's our next move?" Serena asked.

"Let's go to the abandoned training center Nessa visited earlier," Marlys said. "It's closer to the Meadowlands than we are now and gives us options whenever Nessa moves again."

Training centers, in all regions, generally consisted of longhouses of various lengths and widths. A few private rooms, largely for the senior instructing sorcerer or visiting high sorcerers, stood side-by-side at one of the corners. Otherwise, there was a common area for sleeping: one place for apprentices, another for sorcerers. Both had sturdy, comfortable beds and places for each person to store belongings. For the most part, sorcerers retained few personal items.

Elsewhere, residents could make use of a common cooking and dining area. A central brazier and flue normally stood at the center of a longhouse. The surrounding area was generally used in daytime for instruction, or in the evening for entertainment, which could be dancing, games, reading, or conversation. Another fairly large room housed bathtubs. Privies might be inside or out. Wells often were found outside. Water pumps could be located in cooking and bathing areas.

Outside, residents would generally find a barn for animals. Inside, residents might find closets and cupboards for clothes, food, and other essentials.

When they arrived, they unhitched the horse from the cart and led it to a stable. The horse had the barn to itself, and plenty of fodder, kept fresh by sorcery, to eat.

Once inside the longhouse, they carefully checked the rooms. All seemed dust-free. They looked inside cabinets, tested the pumps, lit the lamps, and surveyed the kitchen.

"I'll give them credit for this," Tir said. "They left the place neat, clean, and organized."

Rochelle walked around. "No traps set for us that I can see."

"She wouldn't," Marlys said, "in case she wanted to return."

"And she would want to be sure not to do anything that might harm other sorcerers who might come here in the future," Serena added.

"I'll check the closet for another change of clothes," Tir said. "I don't have an extra set now."

Marlys reflected, not for the first time, that sorcerers and apprentices were fortunate that the people of the region who donated clothes provided a variety of sizes. A large person such as Rochelle as well as a man such as Tir could find outfits that were suitable for their frames. Frequently the donated clothing tended to be loose-fitting. Once in a while, a sorcerer might go into a town and trade for tailored clothes, but generally, sorcerers used never-forgotten household spells to make small adjustments to whatever they wore.

While Tir searched through the clothing, Serena and Marlys went to the kitchen and started supper. Rochelle set the table. They all sat and ate a hearty meal, cleaned up, and relaxed around a fire that Tir had kindled.

The next day, once they had breakfasted and washed up, Marlys cast a locator spell. "Nessa has moved to Valleyview."

"Our home?" Tir asked.

"Our home." Marlys said. As high sorcerer, she spent most of the time at the fortress. But the training center outside the town of Valleyview was where she had been apprenticed, and where she first started training her own apprentices. The longhouse there had been greatly expanded since she had first come to it, now housing over thirty apprentices and sorcerers at a time. She still thought of it as home, as did Tir, Rochelle, and Serena.

"She must know we're here," Serena said.

"Perhaps she thinks we'll follow her," Rochelle said.

"We will," Marlys said. "Zaria, at least, knows our attachment to it and that we will take any strike against it as a personal affront."

"Could we be walking into a trap?" Rochelle asked.

"No more than we have been so far," Marlys said. "We have numbers, experience, and strength on our side."

"Sometimes, sadly, that's not enough," Tir said.

"All we can do is our best," Marlys said.

Upon arriving at Valleyview, Marlys drove the horse cart to the only inn the town had. The building had two stories and was almost the size of the longhouses. They handed the horse and cart over to the attendant at the inn's stable and walked to the front of the inn.

The double door had been left open. Marlys walked in and was immediately greeted by the innkeeper, Filix. He scurried toward the entrance and they met in the middle of the main room, filled with tables that were partially or fully occupied. Most of the patrons looked up when the sorcerers entered. Marlys noticed they smiled or whispered excitedly to each other: the sight of sorcerers visiting an inn was always considered a rare treat.

Filix bowed. "Welcome, High Sorcerer Marlys. There are other sorcerers already here." He gestured behind him. "I gave them a sleeping room and showed them to a private dining room for their meal." His tone indicated he wanted to know whether this was all right with Marlys. Sorcerers sometimes came to inns for meals or to mingle with townspeople, but it was almost unheard-of for them to ask for rooms. Sorcerers generally found lodgings at local training centers.

Marlys nodded. "This was well done. We have an unusual situation. Do you require payment?"

"Never for sorcerers." Filix sounded almost scandalized.

"Would it be an inconvenience to provide rooms for me and my companions as well?"

"Not at all."

Marlys could tell he was being truthful. "Thank you. Meanwhile, we will join the other sorcerers at their repast."

"Food and drink for you and your companions?" Filix said.

Marlys smiled. "Yes. Our usual fare."

Filix nodded, escorted them to the doorway of the private room, bowed, and walked away.

Marlys and her companions stepped inside the room. Tir closed the door behind them. In front of them, Zaria and Nessa sat at a table, eating. They rose when Marlys entered, standing stiffly, throwing her an icy glare.

Undaunted, Marlys walked up to Nessa and stood in front of her, looking her in the eye calmly. "Whatever quarrel you have, you have with me. Leave the townspeople alone."

"I have no interest in them," Nessa said.

"Good," Marlys said. "Swear it."

Nessa rolled her eyes and sighed. "Very well."

The two sorcerers pressed their uplifted right forearms together and clasped hands.

Marlys felt Nessa grip her hand hard, and grasped Nessa's hand with equal force. "Swear that you will do no harm to anyone who is not a sorcerer, or to their properties and possessions."

Nessa lifted her chin. "I swear that I will do no harm to anyone who is not a sorcerer, or their properties and possessions."

Marlys cast the spell to seal the oath with sorcery and released Nessa.

Nessa stepped back. "You lied when you said you did not poison the minds of my friends in the Meadowlands against me."

"I did not lie," Marlys said calmly. "Confirm it with sorcery, if you will." She could sense Nessa applying the spell and remained still.

Nessa let out a huff. "They found out about my releasing the behemoths somehow."

"Oh, please," Rochelle said. "Half the sorcerers at Goldenvalley came and helped us return them to the Looming Mountains. Any or all of them could have used the sorcerous channels to tell the sorcerers at Meadowlands what happened."

"Don't tell us you have never used sorcery to gossip with sorcerers elsewhere," Serena said. "We've all done it."

"However they found out, they found out. I was reprimanded for putting the regions in danger. I explained that I had no intention of doing so and was only trying to cause you grief."

She nodded at Marlys and her companions. "They didn't believe me when I said the creatures would probably have not spread to other regions, and you would have stopped them before that in any case. They didn't accept my explanation. Zaria and I were cast out."

"What a surprise," Tir said sarcastically.

She glared at Tir before turning back to Marlys. "You are the monster here, not me. That should be plain to anyone."

"Apparently it is not," Marlys said. "I have admitted to my mistake and I have long since paid for it."

"Not enough," Nessa said.

"Who appointed you judge of the universe?" Rochelle said.

Nessa turned to her. "I'm the injured party. I have the right to amends."

"My father is a magistrate," Marlys said. "as was his mother before him. What you're doing is not in line with honorable amends. The law does not recognize revenge as a right."

"The civil laws do not apply to sorcerers," Nessa said.

"As I am well aware," Marlys said. "But if you appeal to general law as precedent, then you must accept its limitations. And may I add that when you became a sorcerer, you pledged to abide by the discipline of your High Sorcerer, and the discipline of the sorcerers does not recognize revenge as a right, either."

Nessa turned to Zaria. "Time to leave."

With a withering look to Marlys and her companions, Nessa and Zaria walked past them and left the room.

Filix arrived with platters of food and drink. He displayed his usual polite, pleasant manner and gave no sign he had overheard the sorcerers arguing. The sorcerers sat at the table while the meal was served, thanking Filix for his service and praising the appearance of the food. Once Filix cleared Nessa and Zaria's places, he left the room silently, leaving Marlys and her companions by themselves.

But not for long. They had barely finished eating when sorcerers and apprentices from the training center streamed into the room. There were many merry meetings. Smiles and hugs were generously given and received.

"You didn't think that you could hide here?" teased Voni, the senior sorcerer at the center.

"Obviously, I am not hiding," Marlys said with a smile.

Voni turned to all the other sorcerers. "We've heard from Celestine and the others about Nessa's revenge quest. I'm so sorry that you have to deal with her anger."

Marlys sighed. "Thank you. Though I suppose it was inevitable someone would have come for the ones under my time-binding spell."

"No one with any sense would blame you for casting that time-binding spell on Thorne and her assembly," Voni said.

"Still."

"Are you joining us at the center?" Voni said.

"No, I've taken rooms here," Marlys said. "It would be difficult for me to leave if I were home again."

"We'd protect you if you came home...not that you need protecting," Voni said.

"It isn't that," Marlys said. "This is my quest as well as Nessa's. It is my aim to convince her to relent as much as it is hers to convince me. I need to keep on her trail."

"I understand," Voni said.

In the middle of the night, Marlys awoke at the sound of a commotion outside. She got out of bed, grabbed her cape, and wrapped it over her nightgown. She pushed her feet into her boots as she moved quickly to the door and into the hallway. Tir, Serena, and Rochelle followed, similarly robed.

Townspeople had gathered on the cobblestones in front of the inn, looking toward the training center. Flames shot to the sky and danced there. Sparks and smoke rose into the air with the flames. They heard the distant crackling of fuel, and low cries of alarm.

"They set our home on fire?" Rochelle exclaimed.

"Perhaps something in the forest next to the house ignited," Tir said.

Serena turned to Marlys. "Do we go and help, or do we trust that they can handle this on their own?"

Since the training center was too close to use the distance-shortening spell, Marlys had leaned forward, ready to run toward the blaze herself, but almost as Serena finished her sentence, the flames and sparks died away, leaving only wisps of smoke.

Filix turned to Marlys. "That is why we are all grateful to the sorcerers in the region. A threat forms, and we needn't worry because you take care of it right away."

The townspeople began to disperse. Some lingered for a while to talk with each other, or to acknowledge the nearby sorcerers with a smile or a wave before moving on. Marlys and her companions nodded and waved back.

"Shall we go see what happened?" Tir asked when most of the onlookers had gone.

"I think we could walk nearer and inquire," Marlys said. "But I'm getting dressed first."

"How about trying the sorcerous channels?" Rochelle suggested.

"No," Marlys said, "they're busy handling the fire and its aftermath and we'd just be interrupting. I can't imagine that Voni would not contact us whenever the matter is settled. But we can meet them halfway."

The four sorcerers returned to the inn briefly. Once dressed, they walked down the road toward the training center. Tir conjured a small pillar of light to illuminate their way. The building had just come into view when they saw another light. They could make out Nessa and Zaria approaching, followed by Voni. She had placed one hand on Nessa's shoulder and the other on Zaria's. Behind Voni marched perhaps a dozen sorcerers.

When each group was within a few paces of the other, all stopped. Marlys noted the sullen expressions on Nessa's and Zaria's faces.

Voni turned to Marlys. "We're escorting them out of town. They can get their things from the inn before we send them on their way."

"What happened?" Tir asked. "We saw the fire."

"Celestine warned us that these two might appear suddenly," Voni said. "Since then, we've kept someone on watch at all hours. They surrounded the house with fire. Inside, they used spells to try to demolish sorcerers' belongings."

Rochelle glared at Nessa. "That's your way of causing havoc without violating your oath?"

"We blocked the spells as soon as we realized what was happening," Voni said, "and extinguished the fire. We took these two in hand and I opened a sorcerous channel to Ilse."

Marlys nodded. As Nessa's and Zaria's High Sorcerer, Ilse had the ultimate authority to dole out discipline for them.

Voni nodded to Nessa and Zaria. "In a word, they're banished. They can't return to Meadowlands, and Ilse will inform the High Sorcerers of other regions not to welcome them." Voni indicated the sorcerers behind her with a nod. "Once they leave town, we will shadow them until they are beyond the borders of Goldenvalley. If they attempt sorcery before then, we'll be there to oppose it."

Marlys and her companions walked with Voni and her group back to the inn, where they separated. After extending their farewells, they returned to their rooms, letting Voni and the other sorcerers deal with Nessa and Zaria.

At breakfast the next morning, Tir asked, "What's our next move, now that Nessa and Zaria are banished? Are we rid of them?"

"We have to keep them close," Rochelle said. "We want our friends released from their time-bind."

"I cast a locator spell," Serena said. "They're pursuing their only choice now: they're going to the Spell Passage."

"And we will follow," Marlys said.

Tir smiled and turned to his companions. "That promises to be an adventure."

Part II:
The Spell Passage

Chapter 8

"I've heard about the Spell Passage from the Storytellers," Tir said as he buttered another breakfast roll. "But I don't know anyone who has actually traversed it."

"To my knowledge, no one has for as long as I've been a sorcerer," Marlys said. "Since High Sorcerer Ware and Sorcerer Junia told us they tried to reach the Library of Sorcery, they might have gone through the Spell Passage, though they didn't say so when we were there."

Serena nodded. "When the thought came to me to attempt the Spell Passage someday, I asked around and couldn't find anyone who had gone recently."

"My feeling is that the rare attempts to go through the Spell Passage and then to the Library of Sorcery has less to do with difficulty and more with hubris," Marlys said. "For ages now, sorcerers have felt that they have all the spells they need to know. Few, besides those in our region, even attempt to devise new spells."

"Where do we start, then?" Tir asked. "I know we have to follow Nessa, but I'd rather not do so without any inkling as to where we're going."

"I have little doubt that she is doing it with only the barest knowledge," Serena said. "Therefore, we have the advantage, since I have studied the Spell Passage for years."

"Since you've studied it, Serena, there's something I've been curious about," Tir said. "Why is it called the Spell Passage?"

Rochelle spoke up before Serena could answer. "Because calling it 'the route to the Library of Sorcery which includes stops at sorcerer fortresses along the way' would be tedious?" She grinned.

Tir threw Rochelle an exasperated glance before turning to Serena. "Seriously. Are there spell traps along the way that we need to be aware of? Is the route impassable without using spells? Or is this one of those cases where the name was given in ancient times and no one really knows why?"

Serena smiled. "Your last guess seems to be the case, Tir. I've asked about this myself and have received various answers. Some say that there are unique spells one can learn at the various fortresses which will help find the Library. Others say that there are spell challenges along the passage that test one's resolve to go to the Library. Still others say that 'Spell Passage' simply refers to the fact that the Spell Passage was created for sorcerers. No one seems to know for certain."

"I don't know as much as Serena," Marlys said, "but my sorcerer trainer, Elspeth, despite her many training faults, made sure her apprentices knew the lore of the first sorcerers. They seem to be the ones who established the Spell Passage and named it. So it may well be that the reason for naming it has been lost in time."

Tir and Serena nodded.

Marlys pushed back her chair and stood. "In any event, allow me to show you what I can. Serena can fill in the gaps in my knowledge."

"Show us what?" Tir asked, as Marlys walked to the wall.

Marlys indicated a wall painting. "Filix, as you probably have noticed, has enlisted artists and mapmakers to decorate the walls here with murals. He's able, then, to point out routes to visitors and travelers. This is a map of the continent." Marlys passed her hand over the top of the map. "These are the mountain ranges to the north, where sorcery was said to have originated."

Serena left her chair and waved at the map. "The Shadowmount, where the Library of Sorcery is said to be."

"The Spell Passage winds through paths rarely used now," Marlys said. "It begins where the regional borders end and continues to the Mountains of Wrath and the Shadowmount."

"Wouldn't Nessa go directly to the Shadowmount?" Rochelle said.

"According to our locator spell, she didn't," Marlys said. "She may be daunted by its reputation and try to travel the route of the Spell Passage first, thinking it to be easier."

"Either way contains challenges," Serena said.

"How do we know there's anyone there?" Tir said. "Granted, the tales say that the first sorcerers established stations in the north with repositories of knowledge for sorcery, but I always thought they were long abandoned."

"That's what I've heard," Rochelle said.

"There are traveler's tales," Serena said. "Hunters, treasure seekers have visited the area and stopped at a station along the Passage."

"Treasure seekers?" Tir asked.

Marlys smiled wryly. "Haven't you heard? We sorcerers have treasure stashed all over the continent."

Rochelle laughed. "No one told me!"

"Most know that sorcerers in the here and now have no such hoards," Serena said, "but some still think the ancient residences of the first sorcerers may harbor items of value."

"The only items of value I want to see are spells that will release the time-bind absent the spell caster," Rochelle said.

Serena nodded. "That is the reason we need to follow Nessa and Zaria—to find out."

Tir turned to Marlys. "Maybe if we know Nessa is heading toward a station, we can get there before her?"

Marlys nodded. "We'll try."

Rochelle leaned forward. "Shall we get started?"

Serena turned to Marlys, then back to Rochelle. "We need to gather supplies first."

"Haven't we done that already?" Tir said.

Serena shook her head. "We need to gather additional supplies. Walking staffs. Warmer clothes. We'll have to leave the horse and cart with Voni. There are many places a horse and cart, or even horse alone, cannot go."

"Can't we warm ourselves through sorcery?" Rochelle asked.

"Sorcery can fail." Serena said.

"I've seen spells fail," Rochelle said. "We can't banish a storm. Marlys told Nessa that healing can fail if not applied wisely. But a spell for warmth? I've never seen that fail."

"According to the legends," Marlys said, "there are places along the Spell Passage where sorcery is, at least, unreliable. Try a spell, and it may or may not work, or work in an unintended way."

"Speaking of not being able to banish storms, how's the weather along the Spell Passage?" Tir asked.

"By all accounts, unpredictable, and occasionally fierce," Serena said.

"I can see why the area has been avoided all this time," Tir said.

Rochelle turned to Marlys and Serena. "I agree with what you said earlier, about doubting whether Nessa and Zaria realize what they're facing."

"And yet they proceed anyway." Tir sighed. "Just as they've been doing all along."

"Leaving us to clean up their mistakes," Rochelle said.

"That is the fate of most elder sorcerers," Marlys said, "to remedy the mistakes of the inexperienced. I've had to remedy some of yours, if you recall."

"Yes, but our mistakes were made while we were attempting to help," Tir said. "Nessa and Zaria are deliberately wreaking havoc."

"True," Marlys said.

An apprentice sorcerer came to take the horse and cart back to the training center. Marlys and her companions, relying on Serena's advice, gathered supplies and put them in carry packs. They wore clothes in layers, thinking that if the climate became warmer, they could simply shed the outer garments.

When they were ready, Serena cast a locator spell. "Nessa is heading to Stronghold, the first fortress along the Spell Passage."

Marlys nodded. "Let's get there. We need to make sure that we don't meet them, however. I'll set us a discreet distance away." She cast the spell to shorten distances.

They still had to walk while using the spell. But scenery appeared to fly by. Usually, they knew they had reached their destination when their surroundings looked as they did when proceeding at a leisurely pace.

The distance to Stronghold was long enough for the journey to take at least four days, even with shortening the distances.

Every day each traveling party made one stop for a midday meal and one stop to sleep. Marlys noticed that Nessa halted near towns.

"Probably brought little or nothing with her," Tir said when Marlys remarked on this. "No food, clothes, or bedding."

"Purchasing what she needs or exchanging for sorcerous chores," Rochelle guessed.

When they stopped for their midday meal on the fourth day, Serena cast the locator spell. "It seems Nessa and Zaria finished their midday meal and traveled directly to a place just outside Stronghold. The fortress is now within easy reach of our sorcery."

"I'm taking my time eating, then," Rochelle said.

After their midday meal, Serena cast the locator spell again. "Nessa is still outside Stronghold. Strange that she hasn't moved to the fortress itself. She hasn't moved at all since we arrived here."

"Maybe she and Zaria fell into a clutching bog," Rochelle said.

"Let's find out." Marlys cast the distance shortening spell.

When they reached their destination, Marlys immediately felt snow hit her face. The wind howled around her.

"It seems we arrived in the middle of a blizzard," Tir said.

"You think so?" Rochelle teased.

Marlys turned around. She could see trees close by, but falling snow blocked the view of anything farther away.

Rochelle managed a few steps forward, plunging through the knee-deep snow. "It's difficult, but at least we can walk through...wait, I ran into something."

They all moved closer to Rochelle as she bent down and dug into the snow with her gloved hands. "This looks like—" she dug faster, "—Nessa and Zaria."

Marlys bent to get a closer view. Tir joined Rochelle in the digging, and soon uncovered the two. They had huddled together at the base of a tree. Their eyes were closed. They were not moving.

Tir turned from them to his companions. "They aren't very good at this, are they?"

Rochelle turned to Marlys. "You know, we may find in the end that they've solved our problem for us if they die of their own clumsiness."

"We would have been unprepared if we hadn't had Serena's advice." Marlys bent down and shook them. To her relief, they moved and began to speak, though their words were weak and mumbled.

Tir looked over her shoulder. "I've tried a warming spell, and even a lighting spell. Nothing."

"No results here, either," Rochelle said.

Serena had been slowly turning in a circle, scanning their surroundings. She pointed. "There! I see it!"

Rochelle looked in that direction. "See what?"

"There was a lull in the wind. I saw the fortress at Stronghold: a tall building of gray stone with a crenelated top. It's not far."

Marlys nodded at Nessa and Zaria. "Let's get them on their feet. Serena and I will take Zaria. Tir and Rochelle, you take Nessa."

"I can carry one of them. Might be easier," Rochelle said.

"No, walking will help warm them up," Marlys said.

"Can we drag them through the snow?" Tir asked.

"Snow can drift," Serena said, "especially in wooded areas, there should be shallow spots. Besides, the fortress is close. There's a raised road we should meet within a few steps. The snow will not be deep there."

"Even at short distances, we could get lost in the blizzard," Tir said.

"I'm sure of my direction," Serena said. "And I am seeing glimpses every few seconds. The fortress is so large that if we proceed toward it, we are sure to find it."

Rochelle took off her cloak and wrapped it around Nessa. Marlys did the same for Zaria. Nessa and Zaria were unsteady, but with the support from the others, everyone began to move forward.

As Serena predicted, they soon reached a road. The wind continuously blew the snow off the surface. They followed the path until they reached a set of five stairs. A huge door loomed at the top. They eased Zaria and Nessa down until they sat and leaned against the doorway.

"What do we do now, knock?" Tir asked.

Marlys looked up. "There's a chain hanging down. I'm pulling that."

"Let's hope it doesn't let loose a swarm of stingers," Rochelle said.

"I think she's right," Serena said. "I think this is how visitors announce themselves."

The chain had a brass knob at the end. Marlys gripped it and gave it a hard yank. A loud bell sounded.

Zaria stirred. "I'm cold." Her voice was faint, but clear.

Marlys looked down. "We should be indoors soon."

Zaria pulled Marlys's cloak close around her. "Can't you use a warming spell?"

"Doesn't work here," Tir said.

Nessa looked up at Marlys and her companions. She groaned. "You again. I thought you were just some travelers helping us."

"You're lucky anyone found you," Rochelle said. "Or you might be frozen and dead by now."

"What did you do, find a spell to cancel mine?" Nessa said. "The warming spell didn't work. The protective spell didn't stop the wind. I couldn't reverse the distance shortening spell and go back."

"Our spells aren't working, either," Tir said.

Nessa leaned back, rubbed her hands, and said nothing.

"Shall we try the metal ring to see if the door is unlocked?" Rochelle said.

"Let's wait a little longer," Marlys said. "There are many ways to reinforce doors to repel unexpected visitors which do not depend on sorcery."

At that moment, they heard a thump and scraping from inside. All turned their attention to the entrance. No one said anything, but it seemed to Marlys that everyone held their breath for a moment.

The door slowly ground open.

Chapter 9

A woman stood in the doorway. Marlys estimated that she might be about her own age, perhaps a little older. She wore brown, ankle-high boots, dark green pants, a yellowish-green shirt, and a hat that matched the pants. Her expression was solemn.

She pulled back the door a little more. "I am sorry for the delay. There haven't been travelers here for a long time. I was not expecting you."

Marlys nodded to Nessa and Zaria. "Two of our party are in dire need of warmth."

The woman at the door stepped back. "Come in."

With Nessa and Zaria regaining their senses, it was increasingly easier to guide them inside. Their host closed the door behind them. Marlys felt warmer at once. Stone structures of old tended to be drafty and cold in the winter, but strengthened by sorcery when built, they would retain heat and resist drafts. Some power in the area had inhibited new spells, but such forces would not cancel spells already cast.

"Are you a sorcerer?" Serena asked.

She nodded. "Yes. My name is Gweneth."

Marlys introduced herself and the others. "Zaria is an apprentice. The rest of us are sorcerers," she added.

"Marlys is a High Sorcerer," Tir said.

"I'm afraid I don't know the meaning of that," Gweneth said.

"It means I am responsible for the sorcerers, apprentices, and practice of sorcery for an entire region," Marlys explained.

"I see. The title has little significance here."

"As expected," Marlys said.

Gweneth extended an arm, walked forward, and ushered them into a room where a fire blazed in a stone hearth. Marlys noted that Gweneth seemed to be favoring one of her feet. "Sit and be warm. I'll bring food and drink." She walked out slowly, with an uneven gait.

Marlys and her companions helped Nessa and Zaria into wingback chairs next to the fire. Quilts had been draped across the backs of couches in the room; Marlys and Rochelle grasped the coverings and wrapped them around Nessa's and Zaria's shoulders. Marlys and Rochelle reclaimed their cloaks and sat in upholstered chairs. The others found equally comfortable chairs near the low table in the middle of the room.

Nessa groaned and turned away from the hearth. "Am I to see you everywhere I go now?"

"You're lucky we were there," Rochelle said. "Else you and Zaria might have died out there."

"I don't consider myself in your debt, if that's what you're seeking."

"Unlike you," Rochelle said, "we don't keep a record of indebtedness."

Nessa snorted.

Serena leaned in her direction. "A word of advice?"

Nessa waved a hand.

"I wouldn't argue with us in the presence of any of our present or future hosts. You'll find they are not interested in your righteous quest for justice, and they may become hostile to you if you try to win them over."

Zaria turned to Serena. "Does this mean that you won't try to turn our hosts against us as well?"

"Of course," Serena said.

"Easily done," Tir said.

Nessa and Zaria turned back to the fire.

Marlys and her companions settled in their seats, taking off their carry packs and otherwise making themselves comfortable.

Not long after, Gweneth reappeared carrying a tray.

Marlys looked up. "Would you like help with that?"

"No, I just have to set it down." She placed the tray on the table. A large teapot stood in the middle, surrounded by colorfully decorated ceramic cups. Gweneth sat on the nearest couch, poured tea in the cups, and distributed them.

Tir took one sip and threw his head back. "This is the best tea I've ever tasted."

Gweneth stood, walked over to Nessa and Zaria, and handed them cups. "We grow good tea in the mountains. I tend tea plants myself on these lands."

"I didn't know that one could grow tea here," Tir said.

Gweneth returned to the couch but did not sit. "I'll bring food. Will bread and butter and jam do?"

"Oh, yes, thank you," Rochelle said.

While Gweneth was gone, Tir drained his cup and poured more. He stood and refilled everyone else's cups as well. Even Nessa and Zaria extended empty cups for him to fill.

Gweneth returned with another tray. A large platter held bread, already sliced. A pot with a knife stuck into it contained butter. A similar pot was filled with apple jam. When she set it down, she motioned for the others to help themselves before sitting back on the nearest couch.

Marlys, while waiting her turn, faced Gweneth. "Are you all alone here?"

"Yes. The fortresses along the Spell Passage are all occupied by a single sorcerer. We all ask to be hosts. It's an honor."

Tir finished buttering a large piece of bread and sat. "Do you ever get lonely?"

"No. I don't mind being by myself. Besides, I have the cows, horses, and chickens. I tend the garden."

Rochelle spread jam over bread. "How do you manage such a large fortress without sorcery?"

"I can always use household spells," Gweneth said. "As for sorcery, the glowing orbs come alive only when other sorcerers are present."

"Glowing orbs?" Serena asked.

Gweneth nodded. "In ancient times, following the sorcerous wars, the orbs were distributed among the fortresses along what we now call the Spell Passage to prevent fighting among the sorcerers."

"I'd never heard of those," Serena said, turning to Marlys, who shook her head.

"As far as I know," Gweneth said, "they exist only in the north. They're few in number. Legend has it that they were a gift from the Bright Beings to the first sorcerers."

"May we see them?" Serena asked.

"Yes," Gweneth said. "Later."

Marlys took the tray and held it for Nessa and Zaria to take pieces of bread. When they were finished, she returned to the table, put the tray down, and sat again.

"Would you mind if I asked about your foot?" Marlys said to Gweneth.

"Not at all. I had part of my right foot cut off so that I could be a sorcerer."

Tir nearly choked on his bread. He gulped some tea to wash it down.

Gweneth watched the shocked expressions on Serena's, Rochelle's, and Tir's faces.

Marlys turned to them. "What she is explaining is some of the extreme measures that used to be practiced to transform an apprentice into a sorcerer."

"Hardly necessary," Nessa said. "Some awaken their sorcery by simply wearing a cutting boot."

Gweneth shook her head. "That did not work for me."

"The boot did not work for me, either," Nessa said. "What happened to me is that I was running through a forest in a lightning storm when a tree fell on me. A bear pounced on the branches trapping me. If I had not awakened my sorcery, I would have died by lightning, by bear, or by being crushed. I had several broken ribs and a broken leg to heal afterwards as it was."

"For me, it was escaping a clutching bog," Marlys said.

Gweneth turned to her. "I am impressed. Few escape a clutching bog without sorcerous assistance."

"And that is the reason I had to awaken my sorcerous ability, and at once," Marlys said.

"Thank the Universe we don't do that anymore," Tir said.

Gweneth turned to Tir. "What do you do?"

"We build a crucible—we call it that, though it's more like a stone closet—and reinforce it with magic," Serena said. "To break out without tools requires sorcery."

"It has the advantage of being able to release the apprentice in case of failure, with no harm done," Rochelle added. "I had to try twice before I succeeded."

Zaria turned to the group. "You'll pardon me if I don't quite believe the stories about how hard it was in the past."

"What you do or do not believe does not change what happened," Gweneth said calmly.

Marlys turned to Zaria. "The reason you are skeptical is because the sorcerous community at large has kept these hardships quiet for years. When I was a child, even having a great-aunt as a sorcerer, all anyone outside the training centers knew was that the training was hard. No details, just hard. Because I wanted to be a sorcerer when I was old enough, I just learned everything I could...carpentry, hunting, camping out alone in the woods...."

"None of that would have helped you," Nessa said.

"So my fellow apprentices said when I told them," Marlys said. "I was mocked for it. But I didn't know. I had to guess. Even at the training center, when I was subjected to such cruelty, I was bewildered, thinking it couldn't possibly be necessary to awaken sorcery that way."

"Yes, I remember your stories when I was apprenticed in Goldenvalley," Zaria said. "I only half-believed them even then."

"Too bad you haven't awakened your sorcery yet," Rochelle said. "You would have realized that what Marlys said could actually happen."

"It was only after I time-bound Thorne and the rest that I slowly realized the truth," Marlys said. "In using the sorcerous channels to talk to those in other regions, telling them that I was determined to find another way, I started to hear accounts of apprentices who gave up and went home, some with horrible injuries. Of apprentices who took their own lives in despair. Of delivering remains to grieving relatives and simply telling them that there had been an unfortunate training accident."

"That was cruel," Tir said. "Implying that their loved one simply wasn't strong enough."

"I was turned away from many training centers because they said I wasn't strong enough," Serena said.

"That happened, too," Marlys said. "Still, the regions needed sorcerers. Anyone who seemed able to complete the training was let in."

"Didn't the apprentices who went home tell their friends and neighbors about the training they endured?" Zaria asked.

"Even if they hadn't felt shamed for having to give up on training," Marlys said, "and they did, trainers would bind them with an oath not to say anything about how they were trained."

"I have known many such cases," Gweneth said. "Apprentices who left, or who took on extreme challenges in a desperate attempt to awaken their sorcery and died. Elder sorcerers said they had tried gentler ways and they didn't work." She turned to Marlys. "I commend you for finding one."

"I regret you had to lose a part of a foot to become a sorcerer," Marlys said. "We have not found a sorcerous way to restore a body part once lost."

"I have no regrets," Gweneth said calmly. "I was determined to become a sorcerer no matter what the cost. I would never have been content to stay home and work only household spells. I asked to have part of my foot cut off. Older sorcerers tried to dissuade me. I insisted. The pain was horrific, but to fight against the agony, I had to awaken my sorcerous nature, which caused my entire body to be consumed with pain. It was awful and exhilarating at the same time. I felt spent for days afterward, but in the end, I was a sorcerer." She reached down and touched her boot. "Crafters and healers long experienced with helping those with injuries such as mine were able to make aids for me to wear to compensate. I still have pain at times." She smiled. "But now I'm a sorcerer and quelling my own pain is easily done."

Zaria attempted to struggle out of her chair, failed, and sat back down.

Gweneth stood. "Here. Let me show you to rooms where you can rest."

Nessa had better success in rising out of her chair, but stumbled nonetheless. Serena hurried over and steadied her.

They all followed Gweneth out of the room, Nessa leaning on Serena's arm, Zaria leaning on Tir's. They followed Gweneth at a leisurely pace until they reached a hallway where Gweneth opened doors for them.

Each of the visitors had a large, spacious, well-furnished room. Nessa and Zaria were helped to their respective beds and remained there. Gweneth gently closed doors behind them. After being shown their rooms, Marlys and her companions simply placed their carry packs on tables and rejoined Gweneth in the hallway.

"With so many rooms, there must have been many sorcerers on Passage coming here in the past," Serena said.

Gweneth nodded. "So I believe. Occasionally there were gatherings of sorcerers here, too, I've been told. But these happened in the distant past. Sorcerers on Spell Passage are rare now."

"I wonder if we can see the orbs you described," Marlys asked.

"Of course." Gweneth led the way to a place below ground level, windowless, but not dark. Two large mounds, each shaped like a half-egg, dominated the floor. They glowed yellow and emitted a faint, melodious hum.

As they reached the bottom of the staircase, Tir asked, "Is it safe to walk around them?"

"Completely safe," Gweneth said.

Marlys stepped close to one of the orbs. It was entirely smooth.

"Is it safe to touch it?" Tir asked.

"Yes," Gweneth said. "You'll get the sensation that it's talking to you."

"What does it say?" Serena asked.

Gweneth shook her head. "Nothing in words. Just a sensation."

Tir reached over and put his palm on one. "Warm, but not hot. And yes, it feels as if it's saying something."

Marlys also put a hand on an orb. She felt as if she heard sounds, not through the air, but through her hands. Feelings of reassurance without words being exchanged. After lifting her hand, she turned to Serena and Rochelle, who also touched the orb.

Tir straightened. "Can you lift them? Move them?"

"I have never tried. There's no need to."

"Don't press your luck, Tir," Rochelle said, taking her hand off the orb.

Tir shrugged and smiled. "Just wanted to ask."

"It's enough to know that we can't use sorcery under their influence," Marlys said.

"I've found the interruption of sorcery is not even," Gweneth said. "Even when glowing as they are now, I can occasionally cast spells for a brief time."

"No one has found a pattern?" Serena asked.

"None that I know of." Gweneth turned to the stairs again. "It's time to start preparations for the evening meal, considering I'm not cooking for just myself today."

"We'd be happy to help," Tir said.

Gweneth smiled. "I'll be happy for the help."

They followed Gweneth to a large kitchen. She pointed out the food storage areas and how she wanted supper to be prepared. They all got to work. When the food was ready to cook, she brought out clean pots and pans, placed them on the cast iron stove, and lit a cooking fire.

"No inhibition on household spells?" Tir said.

Gweneth looked up. "None. I can cook and clean as usual."

While supper warmed on the stove, Gweneth showed them the large dining room next to the kitchen. A long wooden table with chairs dominated the room. A cabinet stood at one side.

"I usually eat in the kitchen by myself," Gweneth said. "But with all of you here, we can get out our best plates and eat at the table."

With dinnertime near, and no sorcerous way of summoning them, Serena volunteered to go and bring back Nessa and Zaria. All three returned together by the time the food had been placed on platters and set at the table. They all took seats, Gweneth at the head of the table, Marlys and her companions on one side, Nessa and Zaria on the other. There was little conversation other than requests to pass a plate or a pitcher. Afterwards, they brought everything on the table back to the kitchen for cleaning and storage. Gweneth said she needed to check on the animals for the evening but invited them to take some tea and stored sweets for themselves.

Rochelle filled a tray for her companions; Nessa put together a tray for herself and Zaria. Nessa and Zaria returned to their sleeping rooms; Marlys and the others returned to the room where they had gathered earlier.

After pouring a cup of tea for himself, Tir sat back on a couch with a sigh. "Now that we can speak freely, I want to say I had no idea how brutal training was in your day. I'm glad it's over. If I were you, I would have placed everyone in the Goldenvalley fortress in a time-bind as well."

"The old way of training isn't over in this area, if I heard Gweneth correctly," Rochelle said.

"Word should get around," Marlys said.

Rochelle turned to Marlys. "And High Sorcerer Thorne was completely comfortable with all this?"

"I wouldn't say comfortable," Marlys said. "She saw it as a necessary evil, as did my trainer, Elspeth. As did most other sorcerers and apprentices, for that matter, though I have wondered whether there were some who might have felt pleasure in all that cruelty."

"Inexcusable," Rochelle said.

Marlys sighed. "What I heard is what Gweneth heard, that elder sorcerers had tried kinder methods and they didn't work."

"They weren't trying hard enough," Tir said.

"The better explanation is that they lacked the imagination to visualize another way," Serena said.

"Remember," Marlys said, "it took us numerous attempts and numerous failures before we thought of the crucible that we now use."

"But at least we were trying," Tir said. "They might have tried but gave up and told everyone following them that if it didn't work for them, it was useless to try further."

"I agree," Marlys said, "but we cannot amend the past. All we can do is go forward."

Chapter 10

Marlys had the deepest and most peaceful sleep that night since Nessa had interrupted the wedding ceremony. Due to the orbs, perhaps? Reflecting on that, she thought it was entirely possible that the orbs, left by the kindly Bright Beings to prevent sorcerous conflict, could have calmed her mind. More likely, it was due to their influence that she could be assured that Nessa could not create sorcerous mischief and that she could relax her constant vigilance, at least here, at least a little.

She washed, dressed, and walked to the dining room. Serena, Tir, and Rochelle already sat at the table, dining on bread, butter, jam and shirred eggs.

"Take a seat and join us," Tir said. "Gweneth has gone to bring more milk and tea."

Marlys did so. Soon afterwards, Gweneth came with a tray, sat, and continued eating. Nessa and Zaria appeared after Gweneth had seated herself.

Again, there was little conversation.

When she was finished eating, Gweneth turned to the others. "I have to tend to the animals as well as my usual chores inside. But my main work here is to assist those on the Passage, though I have not been called to do so for many years. What do you need from me today?"

Serena turned to her. "We wish to read any spell books or other writings in your archives, then search for any hidden stashes of spells."

Gweneth nodded. "Whenever you are ready, I will escort you to the library here. But I and others have long hunted for concealed spells, here and at the remaining sites along the Passage. You are welcome to search if you wish, but I doubt that you will find anything."

Marlys nodded.

Nessa put her napkin on the table and faced Gweneth. "We're ready to go to the library now."

Marlys had finished eating and noticed that Tir, Serena, and Rochelle had sat quietly waiting for her. She stood, and everyone else at the table pushed back their chairs as well.

Gweneth turned to the doorway. "Follow me."

Again, they walked through long corridors and up flights of stairs until they reached a large, airy room with a number of large stained glass windows. Marlys saw a wide table surrounded by chairs and a large bookshelf against one of the walls.

Gweneth strode to the shelf, removed a thick book bound in gold cloth, opened it, and set it on the table. "This is our spell book. Among the other books are writings and journals of sorcerers of old. You are welcome to browse anything in the room."

"Thank you," Marlys said.

Gweneth nodded and walked out.

"I'll go and bring up tea and cider for everyone," Tir said, and followed her.

Serena put a hand on the book and turned to Nessa. "We can sit side-by-side and read together. When you've finished reading what's in front of you, put a hand on a corner to signal that you're ready to turn the page. I'll do the same."

Nessa nodded silently and sat. Serena drew up a chair and settled next to her.

Rochelle and Marlys walked to the bookshelf. They browsed through various books. Rochelle grabbed one and took an empty seat at the table. Marlys found what appeared to be a sorcerer's journal and sat next to her. Zaria took her time browsing, but eventually selected a book, grabbed a chair, and settled by a window. Tir returned eventually, placed a tray on the table, selected a book of his own, and joined the readers.

They all sat silently for hours, occasionally pausing to stretch, take a drink, or leave temporarily to use the facilities.

Eventually, Gweneth appeared at the door. "The midday meal is ready."

After eating, again, in relative silence, they returned to the library. Gweneth appeared once more in the early evening to announce dinner. When they had finished eating, Gweneth asked if they needed anything more from her until breakfast the next day. Marlys thanked her and said they needed nothing else that night.

When they had returned to the library and seated themselves, Nessa turned to Marlys. "Now that our host is out of range of our hearing, I have something to say to you."

Marlys looked up. "I'm listening."

"Stop following me."

"You cannot direct my actions, any more than I can direct yours."

"Let me be clear. Until you are ready to release my aunt and the others, I don't want to have anything to do with you."

"That is not a choice you can make. I will remain on your trail for the same reason you want to make my life as miserable as possible: I need you to release my friends."

Nessa huffed a breath and tossed her head. "Annoying me isn't the way to go about it."

"Annoying me hasn't brought you results, either. Have you ever thought of just ignoring me?"

"Have you ever thought of just going away?" Nessa waved at Serena, Tir, and Rochelle. "I have no quarrel with those foolish enough to follow you..."

Tir raised an eyebrow. Serena frowned. Rochelle cleared her throat noisily and pushed back her chair. The legs scraped on the tile as she did so.

"...but I'd prefer to keep you out of sight."

As Nessa finished her sentence, Rochelle walked over to where Nessa was seated, placed her palms on the table, and loomed over her. "Listen, you. I've kept quiet out of deference to my high sorcerer, but I've pretty much had enough of your mindless prattling." She lifted her hand long enough to point at Serena and Tir. "We are not fools. You do not have sole possession of the truth. The sooner that penetrates your thick skull, the better off we will all be. And may I point out that without us, you and Zaria would have frozen to death."

"Storms don't last forever. We were resting."

"Ha!" Rochelle said. "And have you told Zaria that you refused to heal her after she hit her head?"

Zaria turned to Rochelle and pointed to Marlys. "Nessa told me that she was the one that lured the gigantuan to knock me over in the first place."

Tir raised a hand. "That was me."

Nessa nodded at Marlys. "At her instruction."

Marlys turned to Zaria. "I am sorry about that. I didn't think you would be hurt, and I did heal your injury once I saw it."

"Just leave us alone," Nessa insisted.

Rochelle bent down until her face nearly touched Nessa's. "We aren't going anywhere and we aren't taking orders from you. Get used to it." She straightened and returned to her chair.

Before Nessa could reply, Serena turned to her. "Do you want to read the spell books or do you want to spend the evening quarreling? Make a choice now, because you're wasting my time and yours."

Nessa pressed her lips together and turned her attention back to the book.

Zaria returned to her reading.

The remainder of the evening passed in peace. When Nessa and Zaria announced they were going to bed, Serena nodded and closed the book.

"We'll continue tomorrow," she said.

After Nessa and Zaria had gone, Rochelle turned to Marlys. "Despite what Gweneth said, I want to explore the castle. I'm not tired yet."

"I'm not, either," Tir said.

"Why don't the four of us split up," Marlys said. "We'll cover more area that way."

The lanterns in the room had been lit by household spells after sunset. They each took one and walked out. After an hour of exploring, Marlys returned to the sleeping rooms. The others came in soon afterwards.

"See anything?" Marlys asked.

"A lot of interesting architecture," Tir said. "But no spell notes or spell books stashed anywhere."

Serena and Rochelle nodded in agreement.

"It was worth a try," Marlys said.

The next day, near midday, Marlys glanced up from reading another sorcerer's journal and saw Serena close the spell book.

"Anything?" Marlys asked.

Serena shook her head, grasped the book, left her chair and reshelved it. "A few spells that we might try out at home, but nothing that helps us in our current dilemma."

Nessa's face showed her disappointment.

Marlys closed the book she had been reading and looked around. "Nothing I read can help us either. Some very interesting tales, details about the Shadowmount and the Mountains of Wrath, but little that Ware and her assembly hadn't told us."

Nessa turned to her. "You're planning to try to find the Library of Sorcery?"

"If all else fails, yes," Marlys said.

Serena returned to her seat and faced Nessa. "Aren't you?"

Nessa did not reply.

Tir closed the book in front of him. "I've read some very interesting accounts of the history of sorcery. Hard to tell how much is true and how much is legend, however."

Rochelle closed the book she had been reading and pushed it toward the middle of the table. "Same result as you and Tir," she said to Marlys.

Zaria stood, walked to the shelves, and placed her book there. "I learned all the fine details about the life of a high sorcerer, but nothing else." She ambled over to Nessa and sat in an empty chair next to her.

Gweneth stepped through the door. "The midday meal is ready."

Once they were seated, eating a hearty soup with bread and thick pats of hard butter on the side, Marlys said to Gweneth, "We've read what we came for, thank you. We'll be continuing to the next step in the Passage."

Gweneth nodded. "Once you're at a distance from here and I'm alone again, I'll use the sorcerous channels to tell Castlemount that you're coming."

"Do you use them often?" Tir asked.

"Every few days," Gweneth said. "While I don't mind being by myself most of the time, I do miss contact with others. Besides, it is my purpose here to help others on their way, as well as to help anyone in the vicinity in need of sorcerous assistance. That requires knowing what the others are doing."

Nessa finished her meal and nodded to Zaria. "Zaria and I will leave as soon as we gather our things together. We thank you for your hospitality, Gweneth."

Zaria stood from her chair and faced Gweneth. "Yes, thank you. You've been most kind."

The two left the room.

Gweneth turned to Marlys. "You are not traveling together?"

"No," Marlys replied. "Those of us you see here with me are in one group, Nessa and Zaria are a separate group."

"You seemed to know each other well," Gweneth said.

"Yes, we've had previous encounters and our homes are in neighboring regions," Marlys said.

"If I may ask," Tir said, "they spoke of gathering things together, but I don't remember them having any when we arrived."

"They asked for traveling provisions before breakfast. It is part of my task to supply those on the Passage." Gweneth turned from Tir to the others. "Do you need anything?"

"We're not familiar with these lands," Marlys said. "At home, there's enough game and edible fruit and vegetables along the way for a knowledgeable traveler. But I don't know how it is here."

"Sorcerers on the Passage have traveled around without much provision in the past," Gweneth said, "but the supply can be unreliable. It's easier if travelers have food with them."

"How about the weather?" Tir asked. "Do we need more outer clothing?"

"The weather here has always been unreliable," Gweneth said. "We have days when it's hot enough to sweat in the morning, and cold enough for snow in the evening. The snow that you walked through on the way here has already melted. It's pleasantly warm outside at the moment."

"We'll discuss supplies after we help you clean up once we've eaten," Marlys said. "We apologize for being so absorbed in our studies that we haven't helped more in meal preparation and cleanup."

"There's no need to apologize," Gweneth said. "It's part of my task. It's slower if I do it myself, but it gets done and I'm glad to do it."

"We're grateful for all you've done for us," Marlys said. The others murmured assent.

* * *

The fortress had not only a food storage area, but closets and trunks with extra clothes, including shoes and boots, plus equipment such as knives and pots. They took what they needed and stuffed their carry packs.

Marlys asked Gweneth to join them in the front room with the fireplace before they left. Once they were all seated, she said, "What can we expect at the other stations? Do you know?"

"You mean knowledge from the spell books?"

"That and anything else that might teach us something new, especially about the Library of Sorcery."

Gweneth seemed to take a moment to consider. "Castlemount's spell books are little different from ours. Questers who have gone there have remarked about seeing the same spells as they have seen here, according to those charged with the upkeep of that location."

"The books that I have studied about the Passage say there are treasures of value at each location," Serena said.

"That is true," Gweneth said. "It depends on what the sorcerer is looking for. Yvette would be able to give you more information once you arrive at Castlemount."

"One last question," Tir said, "did Nessa or Zaria ask about what was ahead?"

"Only where they could find new spells, or spells that were long unused," Gweneth said. "I told them that Landsmere, the third station, has larger spell books and that many found Stronghold and Castlemount spell books similar. I advised them to stop at Castlemount nonetheless, since sorcerers on the Passage can find help there, as you have here, to speed them on their way. They said that my help was more than adequate, thanked me, and returned to their rooms. They seemed anxious to be on their way."

"Yes, we've noticed they're in a hurry," Rochelle said.

"We're grateful for your help," Serena said. "Is there anything else you can tell us?"

"It is the task of all of us at the stations on the Spell Passage to help as we can," Gweneth said. "But your quest is your own. It is your task to accomplish whatever it was that brought you here."

"As it should be," Marlys said. "We didn't expect you to do our work for us. Thank you again for all you've done."

Gweneth escorted them to the front door and wished them success in their journeys. Marlys and the others exchanged warm farewells with Gweneth before going on their way.

As they walked the path toward Castlemount, Tir said, "My guess is that Nessa and Zaria have gone directly to Landsmere."

"That would be my guess as well," Marlys said.

"An unwise choice," Serena said. "All of these locations were included in the Passage for a reason. The reasons may be unclear to us now and may even be unclear to those currently in charge of each location, but I would not recommend bypassing any of them."

"I agree," Marlys said.

"But what if Nessa finds a spell that releases the time-bind without the spell caster before we do?" Rochelle said.

"Simple. She goes to Goldenvalley and releases Thorne and company. We find the same spell, arrive a few days later and release our friends," Marlys said.

"It may not be so simple once Thorne and her associates are released," Tir said.

"If that happens, we'll manage somehow," Marlys said. "But Nessa may not find an answer before we do, if there's one to be found. Let us not get worried over a situation which may never happen."

"Before leaving that subject, one last thing," Rochelle said. "What if she finds the release spell, and then destroys the page in the spell book so we can't find it?"

"Spell books, especially here, would be protected against that sort of desecration," Serena said.

Rochelle nodded. "Good."

Once they had traveled far enough away from Stronghold so that their sorcery would work again, Serena cast a locator spell. "Nessa, as we guessed, is on her way to Landsmere."

"Then we shorten the distance and go to Castlemount," Marlys said.

Chapter 11

Castlemount proved to be as large and as impressive a fortress as Stronghold, with an equally forbidding front door. Marlys pulled the chain at the side. A bell echoed within. They waited until the door ground open, revealing a tall woman wearing a shirt, jacket, pants, and boots. She smiled.

"You must be the sorcerers Gweneth told me to expect. My name is Yvette. Welcome to Castlemount." She gestured inside. "Please come in."

Marlys led the way up the steps and made introductions as they passed Yvette and stepped into a wide hallway under a high ceiling.

"Would you prefer to see your rooms now or have some refreshment first?" Yvette asked.

"We'd be grateful if you would show us our rooms so we can put down our travel packs," Marlys said. "Then we would welcome refreshment, yes."

"Especially something to drink," Rochelle added.

"Of course."

Yvette led them though long corridors and up two flights of stairs until she came to a hallway lined with doors. She showed each of her guests a room. As with Stronghold, each room was large, clean, and comfortable. They set down their packs and followed Yvette to a large kitchen. A counter in the middle had tall chairs behind it. They sat while Yvette walked to a large pantry with thick walls.

"What would you like to drink? Wine, tea, milk, mineral water? I have several bottled juices."

"Can you pour some sweetberry juice into a glass with some mineral water?" Rochelle asked.

"Of course."

While she was working, Marlys, Tir, and Serena asked for tea. There was already a kettle steaming on the stove. When she had given Rochelle her glass, she took out ceramic cups, prepared the tea, and served it. When that task was complete, she took a chair and sat.

"Thank you," Marlys said after taking a sip. "Very good tea by the way."

Yvette nodded.

"We would like to read any spell books you have," Serena said.

"When you're finished, I'd be happy to show you where they are."

"Do you have glowing orbs here?" Tir asked. "Ones that suppress sorcery when more than one sorcerer is present?"

"Yes. All the stations do. When these fortresses were visited more frequently, it was necessary to prevent sorcerous quarrels."

"Must have been quite a time," Tir said. "I read about it in the books at Stronghold."

Yvette nodded. "I'm glad the days of sorcerous wars are over. Such a waste of time, energy, lives. Sorcery has so many more fun uses."

"I agree with that," Tir said. "With so many centuries of peace, has anyone thought of moving the orbs?"

Yvette appeared thoughtful. "I really don't know. No one has ever tried. I don't know that they can be moved. But it makes me feel safer with them around, and I wouldn't if I could. Nearly all sorcerers I know are friendly, but with complete strangers going on the Spell Passage, who could tell if a rogue sorcerer showed up and tried to cause trouble." She leaned toward them. "Not that I think you would," she added hastily.

Marlys waved a hand. "We understand."

"It works the other way, too," Rochelle said. "Sorcerers coming here wouldn't know if their host was friendly or ill-tempered."

"Quite right." Yvette grinned. "Though I can assure you I'm not the combative sort."

"Even without a spell to verify truth, we can tell," Tir said.

When they were finished, Yvette led them though other long hallways and up more staircases to an enormous room with a large table and chairs in the middle and an even larger table with chairs set against a wall. Tall windows on two sides let in abundant sunlight. She walked to a bookcase, removed a book, and set it on the smaller table.

"We don't have many books here," Yvette said. "Stronghold has more. But this is our spell book."

"This will be fine, thank you." Serena sat in a chair and started reading.

Yvette turned to the others. "We a large number of maps as well, and you're welcome to browse through those."

Tir had been examining the artwork on the walls. "These paintings are breathtaking. Who's the artist?"

Yvette stepped over to the painting nearest Tir. "Painted in the days before the sorcerous wars, preserved by magic, it is said."

Marlys joined them. "This appears to be a mountainous area, windswept, irregular terrain, with patches of snow."

Yvette nodded. "It is said that this is an area near the Library of Sorcery."

Serena paused in her reading to turn to the painting. Rochelle walked over until she stood next to Tir.

"Are there any notes on the painting, in the back, giving it a title or saying what it is? Or are there books with commentary on the artwork?" Tir asked.

Yvette shook her head. "I've checked. My predecessors have checked. It's just a guess passed from station host to station host." She strode to what appeared to be a chest of drawers, a chest much larger in width and length than one for clothes.

She pulled out a drawer. "This is where the maps are kept. I've seen them, of course, but I can't tell you any more about them than what you see on them." She pulled out another drawer. "There are paintings and sketches here, too." She gestured to the walls. "The other paintings are equally mysterious."

"And equally lovely to look at," Marlys said.

"I need to start cooking for our supper," Yvette said. "You'll find me in the kitchen if you have questions."

"Do you need any help?" Tir asked.

Yvette shook her head. "I don't cook often for guests, but it is my pleasure to do so...and my task to leave you to your quest."

"Thank you," Marlys said.

When Yvette had gone, Serena said, "I'll start with the spell book, but I want to look at the maps, too."

"We can stay here as long as we wish," Marlys said. "We won't leave until you've had a chance to examine the maps."

Serena nodded and started to read.

Rochelle walked to the bookcase. "There aren't a lot of books here, but I'll page through the ones they have in case there's something of interest. I'm not good with maps."

Marlys and Tir carefully removed a stack of maps from a drawer and placed them on the larger table.

Tir lifted a corner of the top map and checked the underside. "No writing, no notes." He released the corner. "Not even a signature of the map maker."

Rochelle turned to them. "Could there be secret or sorcerous writing hidden on the paper?"

Marlys glanced in her direction. "Something to ask our host at dinner."

"Would she tell us if there were?" Tir asked.

"I have the feeling they're obligated to answer our questions," Marlys said. "Completely."

Tir turned his attention to the paper. "This looks like a builder's plan."

"For a very large building," Marlys said. "There's at least a scale in the corner."

"How many levels?" Tir asked.

"There's usually a notation in the square with the scale." She carefully flipped through the papers underneath. "No other building plans here." She turned back to the drawing on top. "No staircases or indications of openings in the floor or ceiling."

Tir passed a hand over a section of the plan. "This looks like a kitchen. Dining area next to it. The smallest rooms could be lavatories."

Marlys pointed. "Bathing or washrooms there. A number of rooms in one section of equal size. Probably bedrooms. Larger rooms next to the front and back doors could be places to sit, gather, and talk. Two rooms of enormous size. One could be an audience room. The other could be...," Marlys turned to Tir, "...a library."

"Plans to the Library of Sorcery?" Tir mused. "Here?"

Marlys shrugged. "Just a guess on my part."

"If true, why keep it so far away?" Tir said.

"It makes sense to keep the plans separate," Marlys said, "When the stations for the Spell Passage were built, there was probably frequent travel between here and the Library of Sorcery."

"If it exists," Rochelle called from where she stood at the bookcase.

Serena looked up briefly from the spell book. "There could have been a number of copies made."

Marlys nodded. "Or these could be plans to a completely different place."

"It's not this place, and not anywhere I know of," Tir said.

Marlys turned to Tir. "Ready to continue?"

They carefully placed the top document to one side.

"Now, this looks like a landscape sketch," Tir said. "Trees, rocks, and what appears to be the entrance to a cave."

Marlys lifted a corner of the paper to check the one below. "Look. An indication that this is the first of two documents, and underneath, an indication that this is the second of the two."

They moved the current top paper aside so that they could view both at once.

"The second one is a cross-section of an underground area," Tir said.

Marlys pointed. "They match. See? Here's the place on the diagram that matches to the cave entrance here."

"An underground storage area?" Tir said.

Marlys nodded. "Yes. I've seen similar plans made by winemakers, cheesemakers, anyone who needs a place cool and out of the sun." After closer examination, she added, "This doesn't look very stable, though. These marks indicate holes in the cave floor."

"Places to avoid," Tir said.

"Yes, and look." Marlys lifted the paper so Tir could see the one below. "This map corresponds to the other two sketches, showing the terrain around the cave entrance. Nearby rivers or streams. Stalactites in the second sketch would indicate water leakage. The place could be prone to flooding, ceiling collapse, any number of dangers."

"A warning to be wary of this place?" Tir said.

Serena looked up again. "Or a place that can only be safely navigated with the help of sorcery that would be used to hide valuables. On my way from Majesticacres to Goldenvalley, I stopped at a couple of training centers that used caves for such purposes."

"Is this anywhere around here, I wonder?" Tir said.

"Another question to ask our host," Marlys said.

They placed those papers aside to expose the last paper in that stack.

"This looks like a hunter's map," Tir said. "A map of an area showing where certain animals can be found."

"Yes," Marlys said. "Gigantuans here, fellwolves here...."

"No behemoths indicated," Tir said.

"Sheep herds, goat herds," Marlys said.

"Nowhere I've ever been," Tir said.

"Me, neither."

They carefully put the maps back and pulled out another drawer. Once those papers were on the table, they looked them over.

"This is obvious," Tir said. "Stations along the Spell Passage."

They put that one aside to view the next one.

"The area south of the stations," Tir said.

Setting that one aside, they examined the next one.

"This is north of the stations," Marlys said. "See, they're at the bottom."

"Now we're getting to unknown territory," Tir said.

"Let's keep going." Marlys set that one aside to look at the next one.

"One large map in sections, showing increasing distances north of here to places I'm completely unfamiliar with," Tir said.

"Last one in the stack." Marlys pulled that out. It highlighted a wide, flat area near the summit of the largest height in a mountain range. She placed her hand next to it and turned to Tir with a smile.

"The Library of Sorcery."

Chapter 12

Serena left her seat and walked over to the table where Marlys and Tir had placed the maps. Rochelle, book in hand, strolled over to join them.

"Do you really think that's the Library of Sorcery?" Tir said.

"This corner of the map shows the Shadowmount and the Mountains of Wrath," Marlys said. "We may not know the area around the Spell Passage, but the area around Shadowmount is known to sorcerers in the regions we're familiar with. Ware and members of her assembly knew of it." Marlys waved a hand to the left of the paper. "It seems strange to us only because the maps we have show the approach from the southwest, which is not on these maps, which show the approach from the southeast." She placed a forearm on the map near the left edge. "The part from my arm to the end of the page should look familiar."

The others nodded or made sounds of assent.

Rochelle turned to Marlys. "Then we know how to get from here to the Shadowmount."

"We do now," Marlys said.

"Do you think Yvette will let us take these maps with us?" Tir said.

"No," Marlys said.

"Once I see a map," Serena said, "I can recall it at any time."

Marlys nodded. "My map memory is usually reliable as well. Serena, we can leave these out for you to examine later."

"I can do that now," Serena said. "Even though I'm not able to read sorcerously here, a quick scan shows that Gweneth was right: there are no spells here that we haven't seen before." She lifted a finger. "But there was this." She walked back to the desk with the spell book. The others followed.

Serena sat, opened the book until it lay flat on the table. "I was turning pages when I noticed that the bookbinder placed a flap at the bottom of the book's spine." She glanced up at the others. "As you know, Majesticacres is famous for its bookbinders and printers. My family is in the business. Sometimes the binder puts a fold-in flap for scholars to insert notes or additional material after the book is published. It's not noticeable unless the book is carefully examined or the reader knows where to look." She carefully reached in and drew out a folded paper. After unfolding it, she scanned it quickly. "This is a note saying that we need to have a sorcerous key from here to unlock the spell book at Landsmere." Serena placed the paper on the table. They all bent over it.

Marlys read the paper. "I see. We can't conjure a spell while under the influence of the spheres. But existing sorcery will still be in force."

"Where do we find the key?" Tir asked.

"We can start by looking in this room," Marlys said.

Serena pointed to the chest. "Drawers have been known to have false bottoms. Let's check there to start."

They pulled out the drawers as far as they would go. One did not pull out all the way.

Serena crouched down and looked in. "There's a small drawer in the back." She reached in, pulled it out, put a hand into it, and removed something. She held it up for them to see.

"A piece of metal. Shaped like a snowflake," Rochelle said. "There are several identical pieces there."

Marlys nodded. "I've seen sorcerous keys shaped like this before. We probably only have to touch it to the spell book to open it."

"Can we be sure that this is the key?" Tir asked.

"We can ask Yvette," Marlys said. "Once we've found it, I'm sure she'll confirm it."

"One thing is for certain," Rochelle said. "Nessa and Zaria don't have it."

Tir laughed. "Then Nessa and Zaria will have to return here to get it. Serves them right for trying to skip a station."

"We need to be on the watch for other incentives not to overlook any station on the Passage," Marlys said.

"Was there anything we missed at Stronghold, I wonder," Rochelle said.

"My guess is that there isn't," Serena said. "Whoever thought of the Spell Passage probably made the first station deliberately easy so as not to discourage sorcerers from starting."

"I think we can count on increasing difficulty as we continue, though," Marlys said.

Rochelle grinned. "What's the point of a quest if anyone could complete it?" She walked to a chair, sat in it, and continued to read.

Serena placed the paper with the unlocking hint back in the book before joining Marlys and Tir in examining the maps and sketches. The remaining sketches in the drawers portrayed assemblies of sorcerers, or sorcerers at work.

"Seems little has changed through the ages," Tir said.

Serena pointed to a figure in one of the assemblies. "That seems to be a male sorcerer."

Tir leaned closer to the sketch. "I believe you're right."

Marlys put a hand on his shoulder companionably. "You are indeed the latest in a line of legendary sorcerers."

Tir smiled.

Rochelle finished paging through the books and reported that she found nothing new. She watched as the others replaced the maps and sketches.

With that task done, they all turned to examine the paintings on the walls. Each occupied a space comparable to a large window.

As they strolled from painting to painting, Serena said, "I wonder if these are all paintings of the landscape around the Library of Sorcery."

"Would be nice if one of these was of the library itself," Tir said.

Serena smiled. "Oh, that would take the mystery out of it, wouldn't it?"

"Does everything have to be a mystery?" Tir said.

"My guess is that even long ago, they didn't want just anyone walking into their most valuable sorcerous repository," Marlys said.

After looking over one particular painting, the others walked to the next one as Tir lingered.

Serena looked back at him. "Something?"

Tir rubbed his chin thoughtfully. "A very small item on the painting here. Something about it...."

The others walked back to join him.

"Which one?" Marlys asked.

Tir pointed.

Rochelle moved closer to the painting. "I just thought that was a hunter's shelter." She turned to the others. "Like the one we were at earlier."

"No, but the shape reminds me of the building plan we took out at the beginning," Tir said. "This could be that building, seen at a great distance."

"The Library of Sorcery," Serena said softly.

"Now that you mention it," Marlys said. "I see the resemblance, too."

"But far enough away so that the details aren't clear." Rochelle sighed. "Another mystery."

"Yes," Marlys said. "We hope all of these are of the Library of Sorcery, and they may well be, but we have to remember that these could be picturing something else altogether."

"Wouldn't that be disappointing," Tir said.

By the time Yvette came back and announced dinner, they had examined everything in the room.

As they approached the dining area, Tir said, "Mmmm, I smell fresh baked bread."

Yvette smiled. "Yes, I take great pride in my baking."

When they reached the dining room, they found the table set. Filled bowls and platters were within reach. There was roast chicken, potatoes, sweetfruits, and other delicacies.

After they had been seated and served, Marlys turned to Yvette, who sat at the head of the table. "We have some questions, if you don't mind."

"I'm here to answer them, if I can," Yvette said.

"First of all," Marlys said. "Is there any secret or sorcerous writing on the maps, drawings, or artwork we saw in the library?"

Yvette shook her head. "No. Knowledge of any sorcery at this location is passed down from station host to station host. I wish to add that I've checked those papers myself to satisfy my own curiosity. So, no."

"You said that you don't know what the maps and plans and sketches and paintings portray," Marlys said. "But I wondered if there was any speculation that anything there points to the Library of Sorcery."

"Oh, there's speculation," Yvette said. "I've wondered myself. But again, nothing certain has been passed down to me or recorded. Your guess is as good as mine."

"I found a slip within your book of spells," Serena said. "It said we have to have a key to open the spell book at Landsmere." She reached into a pocket and brought out the snowflake-shaped object. "Would this be it?"

Yvette smiled and nodded. "It is. Those who founded the Spell Passage set out challenges and discoveries at each location, except the first. It's my understanding that this is to test the questers, and also to train their minds to solve problems."

"Does that mean that the designers intended the Spell Passage to train sorcerers?" Marlys said.

"What we understand," Yvette said, "is that the Spell Passage is for sorcerers looking for new spells, or hoping to enhance their sorcery. It has also been passed down to the station hosts that the Spell Passage is to ready the questers to visit the Library of Sorcery."

Tir paused in lifting a spoonful of sweetberries to his mouth. "Does that mean there's a penalty to those who haven't been prepared?"

Yvette shrugged. "I don't know for certain. Nobody does. But that is the opinion shared by me and the other current hosts, as well as past hosts."

Serena turned to Yvette. "You said you keep records of questers?"

"Yes, there's a large book in the station archives. We don't keep such records in our library or where questers can easily access them."

"Then we're forbidden to see them?" Marlys asked.

"Not forbidden. I can show them to you if you wish. But we don't offer them or leave them out where anyone can see them."

"Did Stronghold list us in their records?" Rochelle asked.

"Undoubtedly," Yvette said. "Every station you visit on the Spell Passage will record that you have visited."

"Would you be willing to show us those records?" Marlys said.

"When we've finished eating and after I've cleaned the kitchen for the next meal, yes," Yvette said.

"How is the Spell Passage knowledge passed from predecessor to current host?" Serena asked.

"Whenever possible, the retiring host stays on for a time to train a successor," Yvette said. "That happened to me. There's also a book where station hosts write what they believe their successors ought to know."

"Is it possible for us to see those books, too?" Marlys said.

Yvette nodded. "I'll show them to you when I show you the visitor records. They're in the same room."

"What happens to the hosts who retire?" Tir asked.

"They go to a nearby town and move into the sorcerers' residence there. We don't have anything like a palace for high sorcerers as the regions do. Just a large building designated for sorcerers to live. We're few in number here, so the domiciles aren't crowded. We get along well."

After they finished eating, everyone pitched in washing dishes, storing leftovers, and cleaning the kitchen.

Yvette led them through corridors to a door with an ordinary lock. She produced a key, unlocked it, and opened the door. They walked into a small room, well-lit by light coming through tall windows. A writing desk and chair stood next to shelves of books. The desk surface was angled with a narrow tray at the top for an inkwell, quill, and knife to trim the quill. At the bottom, a gutter angled upward would keep papers from slipping off the desk surface.

Yvette took a thick book from the shelves, set it on the desk, and sat in the chair behind it. The others gathered behind her. She opened the book at the beginning.

"As you can see, there's just a list of names at first. No dates on these pages, not even yearly notations." She turned pages until she had progressed through about a quarter of the book. "At this point, the lists are arranged by year." She kept turning pages. "Quite a number of names each year at the beginning of the yearly reckoning, then slowly tapering until only a few names per year in recent years."

"Or none," Tir observed.

Yvette nodded. "There have been years when no one came, yes."

"I noted some legendary names of sorcerers at the beginning," Marlys said.

"Or sorcerers named after legends," Serena said.

Yvette turned to her. "True, and I have no way of telling which of those applies."

"Can I see the most recent pages again?" Marlys asked.

Yvette obliged.

"See anyone you know?" Rochelle asked.

"A few. Can I see that last page again?" Marlys asked.

Yvette turned the page.

"Yes, I thought I saw that." Marlys pointed. "Thorne. And Elspeth."

"According to the years given, at much younger ages," Tir said.

"They never mentioned going to the Library of Sorcery, however," Marlys said.

"I don't know of anyone who has," Yvette said. "They complete the Spell Passage and go home. Or they don't complete it at all. A fair number quit in the middle."

"In my travels from training center to training center," Serena said, "I heard several times that sorcerers would go on the Spell Passage just to brag that they did it."

Yvette nodded. "That is true. If you complete the Spell Passage, you'll receive a small coin."

"I never saw one on Thorne or Elspeth," Marlys said. "Then again, I wasn't looking for one, either."

Yvette turned the collar of her shirt. "It looks like this."

They saw a small round coin with the imprint of an open book on it.

Yvette turned her collar again. "I had it made into a pin so I could wear it. Others have crafters make them into buttons or wristlets."

"Possibly Thorne and Elspeth had theirs similarly hidden," Rochelle said.

Marlys nodded and turned back to Yvette. "Another question. You said that you don't know anyone who reached the Library of Sorcery after completing the Spell Passage. How can you tell?"

Yvette stood and grabbed the book of visitors. She went to another shelf and brought back another thick book to the desk. After sitting again, she opened it.

"It's in the book of lore that station hosts pass from one to the other. See?" She pointed to a note on the page. *Those who have been at the Library of Sorcery radiate a sorcerous aura that other sorcerers can view.*

Marlys inclined her head. "I saw Thorne and Elspeth after I become a sorcerer. Neither had an aura."

"Besides," Tir said, "if you had been to the Library of Sorcery, could you resist telling everyone you knew?"

They all chuckled.

Marlys pointed to the book. "Is there any objection to our reading this?"

Yvette closed the book. "Yes. I said that I would show it to you, and I have. But I don't give it out to read."

"Forbidden knowledge?" Tir asked.

"No. Station hosts consider it too precious to place in the hands of others. If I made an exception and let one person read it, I would have to allow anyone who asked to read it. This has to last for generations. Even with sorcerous protections, I would not feel comfortable handing it to anyone but another station host or a successor."

"Fair enough," Marlys said.

Yvette smiled. "Besides, this book has the spell used to create the snowflake keys you found. We keep that knowledge to ourselves."

Serena nodded. "Understandable."

Yvette grasped the book and stood. "I'll put this back and ask you to leave the room ahead of me."

"Of course," Marlys said. They filed out.

After Yvette closed the door and locked it behind her, she turned to the others. "Is there anything else I can help you with this evening?"

Marlys turned to her companions. "No, we'll just retire to our rooms. We'll see you in the morning."

The next day, after breakfast, Marlys asked Yvette if it would be allowed for them to explore the castle.

"Yes," Yvette said. "Any room you may not enter will be closed to you. That includes my own rooms."

By the time of the midday meal, they had checked every open room in the castle. They found it much the same as the fortress at Stronghold and agreed that they had been sufficiently thorough and were ready to continue.

After the midday meal, they thanked Yvette warmly and returned to their rooms for their carry packs. Yvette escorted them to the door and wished them well on their journeys. "I'll tell Clea at Landsmere to expect you," she said in parting.

Once they had walked far enough away from Castlemount, Serena cast the locator spell. "Nessa and Zaria are on their way back to Castlemount."

"Let's not cross paths with them," Marlys said. "Cast a distance shortening spell that avoids them."

Serena did.

Chapter 13

The Landsmere fortress looked similar to Stronghold. Clea opened the door almost immediately once Marlys yanked the chain. "Please come in. I've been expecting you."

When Marlys reached the top of the stairs and walked inside, she saw that Clea's height was about three-quarters of her own. Clea had dressed formally, as if for a gathering of sorcerers, in expertly-tailored clothing.

After closing the door behind them, Clea led the way to a room with a blazing hearth, an artistically woven rug, and a low table surrounded by couches and chairs. The table held a teapot and teacups. "Please have a seat," she said, taking the teapot and beginning to pour. "Set your things anywhere for now. I'll show you to your rooms after we've had the chance to get acquainted."

Marlys and her companions set their packs on the floor. Each found a place to sit. Clea distributed the filled teacups. When everyone had a teacup, including herself, Clea settled into an elegantly upholstered chair which fit her comfortably. "Welcome. Yvette described you, so I know who you are. I presume they told you my name?"

"Clea. Yes," Marlys said.

"Pleased to make your acquaintance," Clea said. "I presume you'll want to read the spell book here?"

"Yes," Serena said. "We have the key to open the book."

Clea grinned. "Good. Not everyone who comes here does." She took a sip of tea and put the teacup on the wide armrest. "Did you want to start today or rest first?"

"If you can show us where to store our carry packs first, and then show us where the spell book is, we'd be much obliged," Marlys said.

Clea rose from the chair and led the way to rooms comparable to those they had at Stronghold and Castlemount. After that, she led them to a large room with a table in the middle, surrounded by chairs. Although there was a library ladder to reach the highest shelves, not unusual in any library, Clea walked to a lower shelf, retrieved a thick book, and set it on the table.

"This is our spell book. You can read this or anything else on the shelves."

"Any others you would recommend?" Tir asked.

"Depends on your purpose," Clea said. "If you're here for spells, this is the book you want. If you are interested in histories or journals of various sorcerers, we have those too."

"Thank you," Marlys said.

Clea nodded. "If you have questions, I'll be in the kitchen. It's down the stairs and to the right."

"We're willing to help with cooking or cleanup," Tir said.

"As for cooking, I had just about everything ready before you came. I'd welcome the cleanup help, however. Thank you for your offer. Not everyone does." She turned to leave but paused at the door. "I'll return when dinner's ready."

When she was gone, Rochelle turned to the others. "Why do I have the feeling that 'not everyone' refers to Nessa and Zaria?"

"Both in the reception room and here, yes," Marlys said.

Serena took a seat and placed the snowflake-shaped key on the book. The key dissolved into ash and the book opened on its own. She started reading. The others took books from the shelves and sat at other places on the table.

When Serena had paged through nearly all of the book, she stopped and looked up. "A new spell!"

The others closed their books, left their seats, and clustered around Serena, reading over her shoulder.

"A calling spell?" Tir said, turning to the others.

"Yes, it appears to be," Serena said.

They all silently read the spell. Eventually, Serena, Tir, and Rochelle turned to Marlys.

"I haven't seen or heard of a spell like this, either," she said. "It's too bad we can't cast a spell here, or we could try it out right away."

"Dinner's ready." Clea said from the doorway.

The others turned to her. "Can you tell us more about this calling spell?" Marlys asked.

Clea walked over, stood with her side to the table, and glanced toward the book. "Oh, yes, the calling spell."

"Is it like the sorcerous channels?" Rochelle asked.

"Not exactly," Clea said. "To speak through the sorcerous channel, you need to know the identity of the one on the other end, and the party at the other end has to be a sorcerer. This is like shouting, only through magic."

"Anyone can hear?" Tir asked.

Clea nodded. "You hear through your head, not your ears, though."

"You can call anyone?" Tir asked.

"Yes. People, animals. I find it useful if one of the animals here is lost or strayed. They come running right away. For people, though, they can ignore it, just as one can ignore a voiced shout."

"Does it sound like a shout through your head?" Marlys said.

"No, the call is at a comfortable level. It doesn't manifest as words, but you know who's calling and where they're located. You can come if you wish. It can get annoying, though, if the sorcerer casting the spell keeps calling."

"Can you shut it off?" Tir asked.

Clea reached over and turned a couple of pages. She rested a fingertip in the middle of a page. "Yes. That's the spell that does it."

"Does it have a distance limit?" Marlys asked.

"The horizon," Clea said. "And it is directional. The call will go out in the direction you're facing."

"Exact direction?" Tir asked.

"No, it doesn't have to be a narrow direct line," Clea said. "It's the width of your view when you face forward."

"But you could turn from side to side and keep calling," Rochelle speculated.

"Yes," Clea said. "You can do that."

"Do you use the spell often?" Marlys asked.

"Not often. The sorcerers in this area consider it a minor spell. Again, it's most useful for animals."

"Thank you." Marlys turned to Serena. "Leave the book open and we'll return to it after we've cleaned up after dinner."

* * *

Clea took a seat at the head of the table. Her custom-made wooden chair had decorative cushions on the seat and back.

"I'm impressed with your personal furniture," Marlys said.

"Thank you," Clea said. "I made all of them myself."

"Your crafting technique is quite artistic," Serena said.

"Again, thank you. I've had years of practice. I started almost as soon as I could hammer a nail. Adapting other furniture or having others make furniture for me didn't give me the comfort I wanted."

"I learned carpentry myself," Marlys said. "I thought that it was best to learn a number of skills in order to become a sorcerer."

"Carpentry isn't a requirement, even here. Hilde, at the fifth station, can fix very little except through sorcery. She has a carpentry family come from the nearby town to help her with tasks that sorcery can't address. Most of us can do some carpentry, however. We all can cook, though some of us are better at it than others."

"Cooking seems to be highly valued among sorcerers," Marlys said. "About the only compliments I received where I was training were for my cooking."

Clea turned to her. "I'm getting the sense you weren't treated well?"

"To say the least," Marlys said. "Before my sorcery awakened, I was constantly trying to defend myself though household spells, such as by pinching others."

"Did it work?" Clea asked.

"Sadly, no," Marlys said.

"The process of awakening sorcery can be a terrible experience," Clea said. "Although I've been largely treated well by those around me, both growing up and at my training center. Mistaking me for a child is what I've had to deal with the most. That, and people telling me that I am too cute for words."

"Sorry you've had to deal with that," Serena said.

"Once I became a sorcerer, I had universal respect, from fellow sorcerers as well as others," Clea said.

"Fear of what we might do, or awe of what we can do," Rochelle said.

"There is that," Clea said. "Like many others, my awakening was a traumatic experience. I was an apprentice and felt I could build a better bed than the one they gave me. After I had endured it for what I felt was too long, I went into town, alone, to get materials I couldn't get around the training center. This was not unusual. I had done it several times before to build myself chairs and other things."

"How did you get the materials?" Marlys asked.

"I was fortunate to be at a training center near a town with a prominent building guild," Clea said. "There was a large storehouse that carried supplies: wood, bricks, nails, hammers, saws, just about anything a builder might need. They donated what I needed since I was an apprentice sorcerer. The owner and I would talk about the craft of furniture making. I learned a lot from him."

"You awakened your sorcery there?" Tir asked.

Clea nodded. "I walked into the storehouse and saw three men I hadn't seen before. I didn't see the owner at first, but looking around, I saw him tied up and gagged."

"Robbery?" Marlys asked.

"Yes. Before I could do anything else, they grabbed me and dumped me into a wooden storage box with a lid."

"Anything in there?" Rochelle asked.

"Empty. The owner sold such wooden boxes, and this was one of those for sale. They piled bricks and planks on top so I couldn't get out. When I yelled, they kicked the box and told me to be quiet."

"How long were you in there?" Tir asked.

"Long enough. I could hear the three men moving around, talking about what they should take. I was getting hungry. It was the heaviest day of my period. If I didn't get back to change my rags, I would have started bleeding all over my clothes and I'd have to either clean them or make more clothes. Did I mention that I had to get good at sewing and altering garments as well?"

"No," Marlys said, "but I was admiring your clothes and wondering who put them together."

"Me," Clea said casually. "So you can see now why I wanted out as soon as possible. I wanted out even more when the lid started to sag from the weight of the bricks. I yelled again, but they only kicked the box again. I strained and strained and strained with all my might. Pain began to surge though my entire body. I pushed against the lid with all I had in me, and more. Suddenly, the lid flew off, the bricks flew off, the planks flew off. The crash was thunderous. I was exhausted, as I'm sure you all remember from your own awakenings. I slowly climbed out of what was left of the box."

"What happened to the robbers?"

"They dodged debris, at first. By the time the dust settled, townspeople had come running to see what the crash was about. Two sorcerers from the training center came in too, wondering why I was taking so long, thinking something might have happened to me. The robbers were apprehended, the owner was freed, and the sorcerers helped me get back home."

"Did you ever get your new bed?" Tir asked.

"Once I recovered from the awakening of my sorcery," Clea said. "The town builders offered to make one for me, but I said that, with all due respect to their skills, I'd rather make the bed myself. They did provide me with an excellent mattress of an appropriate size, however."

"I have been reading journals written by sorcerers here and am constantly amazed by the dire circumstances that sorcerers needed to go through in the past in order to awaken their sorcery," Tir said.

"In the past?" Clea said.

"We have better methods of awakening sorcery in the regions now," Marlys said. "It's still excruciatingly painful and still exhausting, but no longer cruel."

Rochelle gestured toward Marlys. "Marlys has taken the lead in that respect. She's the one who made it happen."

"It's still a horrific experience here, whether by accident or intention," Clea said. "I'd be interested in how you make it happen."

"Of course," Marlys said. "We have the entire rest of the meal, and the cleanup, to discuss it."

When supper was over, they all helped with cleaning up. Marlys noticed that Clea had made several modifications to the kitchen to accommodate her height: stepladders to reach high cabinets, low tables for meal preparations, secondary sinks within her reach, water pumps with extended handles and spouts.

When they were finished, Clea retired to the station host's room, which Marlys presumed was similar to Yvette's, to write down the methods they currently used for awakening sorcery. Clea said that she intended to spread the details to the other sorcerers and training centers in the Passage area. They might use it, they might not, she said, but at least they would have another option.

Meanwhile, Marlys and her companions returned to the library to finish reading the spell book, and to make notes about the new calling spell to take with them.

The next day, after breakfast, Marlys told Clea that they wanted to explore the castle. Clea personally took them on a tour, pointing out interesting aspects of the architecture and giving some of the history of the location. At the end of the tour, they thanked Clea and told her that they would continue on their quest after the midday meal.

"I understand," Clea said. "Though if you wished to stay longer, you would be welcome. Not everyone who comes here is as interesting as all of you have been."

"You've been a most gracious host. We appreciate all you've done for us," Marlys said. "But we have friends at home that need all the knowledge we can muster and our assembly is anxiously awaiting our return."

"What sort of knowledge are you seeking?" Clea asked.

"A way to release a time bind without the presence of the original caster," Marlys said.

Clea raised an eyebrow. "That I do not know. I know of no one who does. You may indeed have to reach the Library of Sorcery to find such knowledge, if it exists at all."

"That's our quest," Serena said.

"Then I wish you all the best with it," Clea said. "If ever you wish to return, please do so. You do not have to be on a quest to visit here."

"We would all be happy to visit you again if circumstances allow," Marlys said. "However, there are a number of pressing issues that require our attention back home, and those may take years to resolve."

Clea spread her hands. "I have all the time in the world."

Marlys smiled. "And there are the sorcerous channels."

"Speaking of which, I'll tell Petra over at Heathervale that you're coming. May the blessings of the Bright Beings go with you."

Once they had traveled far enough away from Landsmere to cast a spell, they found that Nessa and Zaria were on their way to Landsmere.

"Presumably in possession of a sorcerous key," Rochelle said.

"Whether or not they have one, we go on," Marlys said.

Chapter 14

Petra opened the door to Heathervale soon after they pulled the chain and rang the bell. She greeted them warmly, showed them where to set down their carry packs, and escorted them to the library. Once she had given them the location's spell book, she left them to read. She returned with a tray laden with tea and small cakes which she set on the center table.

"Thank you!" Tir said, reaching for them.

Petra smiled. "Is there anything else I can bring?"

"Not right now," Marlys said. "This is more than sufficient. Thank you."

After they had finished the cakes and cleaned the crumbs from their hands with the napkins Petra had brought, Tir raised his head. "Is that a flute I hear?"

Everyone paused and listened.

"Yes," Serena said. "It's a flute, played by someone experienced."

"Shall we stay here and keep reading or become a live audience?" Marlys said.

"We can stay here as long as we need and I can read the spell book anytime," Serena said. "Let's go."

"I'm coming," Rochelle said.

They made their way through corridors and down flights of stairs, following the sound.

"You would think the sound was nearby, but no," Tir said, after they had descended another flight of stairs.

"Sound travels better in some places than others," Marlys said.

One more flight of stairs brought them to a windowless room with a stone floor. Lanterns set in recesses illuminated the walls. Petra stood off to one side, playing a long flute. She glanced in their direction but continued the melody without a pause.

Blocks of stone that appeared to be seats were clustered near a corner. They sat facing Petra as she played on. When she finished and lowered the flute, they applauded.

Petra bowed. "Thank you. I don't often have an audience."

"You wouldn't happen to have a lute, would you?" Tir asked.

Petra gestured toward the room's entrance. "You'll see the door to a room on the left. There's a lute there."

"How about a lyre?" Rochelle asked.

"There are several instruments there. Take what you wish."

"I'll be right back." Tir walked toward the door, followed by Rochelle.

They returned shortly, Tir with a lute, Rochelle with a lyre. They stood next to Petra and tuned the instruments.

"Do you know 'The Flowers In Spring?'" Tir asked.

Petra nodded. "Yes. That's an old one."

Rochelle smiled. "That's why everyone knows it." She held the lute close. "Shall we begin? One, two, three...."

Marlys and Serena sat watching as the others played and applauded when they finished.

"It's been too long," Rochelle said. "I miss my music."

"So do I," Tir said.

"I enjoyed our playing together," Petra said. "As for the instruments, although my task is to assist you, I can't let you take the instruments with you."

"Oh, we wouldn't ask," Tir said. "But would you loan them to us while we're here?"

"Of course," Petra said.

"Shall we start to play whatever comes into our minds and have the others join in?" Rochelle asked.

Petra nodded.

"You start," Tir said to Rochelle. "We'll join in."

They did and played for some time. At one point, Serena leaned over to Marlys and whispered, "I miss hearing music, too."

Marlys nodded.

When they finished, Serena and Marlys applauded and stood.

Petra reached over to a recess in the stone wall. She took out a case and put her flute into it. "I need to start cooking dinner. You're welcome to stay and continue playing if you wish. I come here because the music resonates so well."

"Do you need help?" Tir asked.

"Thanks, but Clea told me you were coming so I prepared for visitors. I only need to heat everything up. I'll give a shout

when it's ready. As you heard, sound carries very well here."
She took the case in hand.

"Your personal flute and not the Heathervale instruments?"
Marlys asked.

Petra nodded. "I've had this since I was twelve." She gave
them a wave and walked out of the room.

"Back to the spell book?" Tir asked.

"We don't need to rush back," Marlys said. "Did you want to
stay and keep playing?"

"I want to try these out in other rooms to see how they sound
there," Tir said.

"I would, too." Rochelle said.

"Don't go without me!" Serena said. "I want to explore the
castle, too."

"How about we go back to the library," Marlys said. "Tir
and Rochelle can keep playing there. Serena and I can read
books."

"I'd rather play than read anyway, if you don't mind my
saying so," Rochelle said.

"Not at all," Marlys said. "It's Serena and I who are primarily
gathering the knowledge."

As they filed out of the room, Tir said. "Since the sound
carries, Rochelle and I could stay here, but just as Serena wants
to explore the castle with us, I want to stay in the library when
you read in case you find a good spell."

"Oh, yes," Rochelle agreed.

They found that Petra was right: they could hear her calling
them for dinner.

"Do we know where the dining room is?" Tir asked as they
left the library.

"In the other castles, the kitchen and library were located
in about the same place relative to the front door," Marlys said.
"We can start in that direction. I'm sure Petra will find us."

"I've noticed that, too," Tir said. "With minor variations, the
floor plans to these fortresses are essentially the same."

"Same architect?" Serena guessed.

"Possibly," Marlys said, "or the builders just saved time and
energy by using the same plan over again."

"Come to think of it, the houses in the towns and villages stick to a few basic plans," Rochelle said.

As it happened, Petra stood waiting for them at the bottom of a staircase and escorted them to the dining room.

After they ate and helped with the cleanup, all four of the visiting sorcerers set out to explore the fortress. Beginning with the highest levels, they worked their way to the underground levels. They quickly scanned the music room, having been there at length before. Another room had the glowing orbs.

Tir crouched next to an orb. He stroked the surface of one affectionately. Turning to the others, he said, "I definitely get the impression it's talking to us."

Marlys turned to Rochelle and Serena. "So do we."

Rochelle nodded.

Serena smiled. "Sometimes these magical artifacts speak directly to the heart."

They walked out together to the last underground room. After descending the stairs to the cold stone floor, Marlys raised her head and looked around. "Anyone else hear singing?"

"Yes," Serena said. "If we stand still quietly we may be able to tell where it's coming from."

For a time, no one moved.

Tir pointed and padded softly toward one of the walls. The others followed.

Marlys saw a yellow glow on the wall at about eye level. Moving closer, she saw a set of saucer-shaped crystals, stacked vertically, in the wall recess there.

"Reminds me of tuning crystals," Rochelle said.

"Or glass bells," Tir said.

Serena leaned sideways toward them, moving her ear closer. "Yes, it does sound like singing."

"No words," Marlys said. "Just 'aaah, aaah, aaah.'"

"I wonder if we could tap them." Tir moved a finger closer. "No, something's preventing me."

"A spell?" Rochelle asked.

"It would have had to have been cast before we arrived," Serena said.

"Maybe from the time the castle was built," Marlys said.

Tir poked the air a couple more times. "No, it's not letting me near." He put his hand down.

"Lovely tune." Rochelle began to imitate the notes with her voice. "Aaah, aaah, aaah...."

Soon the others joined in. After a brief time, the tune started to repeat.

Serena paused. "The crystals are glowing brighter."

Encouraged, all of them started singing louder. Without stopping his part in the song, Tir again extended his hand, and this time was able to touch the crystals. The reverberation became more lively.

Petra walked down the stairs.

They all stopped singing. The crystals song faded into softness again.

"I see you've found the singing crystals," Petra said.

"Yes," Serena said, "is there a spell there?"

Petra nodded. "There is. They vibrate all the time, and there's a spell to keep out contact, except if you sing, and then the barrier dissolves and you can touch them."

"They seem to like it," Tir said.

"Yes, they do," Petra said. "They're like a chorus. I join in with them all the time. We play off each other."

"It was more like a singalong," Marlys said.

"Here, let me show you." Petra began to sing. She had a clear, professional-quality voice. There were still no words, but this time it was more like a four part harmony, with the crystals supplying more than one part.

When she finished, Tir said. "That was delightful."

Petra smiled. "It takes a practiced singer to really bring out their best tones."

"The four of us have voices that are fine for community sings, but not for performance," Marlys said.

"Even so, all of you did very well," Petra said. "Not many can even bring out as much as you did."

"Do they respond to instrumental music?" Tir asked.

"They do," Petra said.

"In that event, let's get the instruments," Rochelle said to Tir.

They spent the remainder of the evening in concert with the crystals.

The next morning, after breakfast, they thanked Petra for her hospitality and started on their journey to Hilltop.

Chapter 15

When the door opened at Hilltop, they saw three children standing at the threshold.

For an instant, Marlys was startled at not seeing a sorcerer. Then she said, "Is Hilde at home?"

The tallest of the children turned and shouted, "Hilde! They're here!"

Marlys and the other sorcerers approached the doorway. The children stepped back as the sorcerers stepped inside. One child closed the door behind them.

A sorcerer walked toward them in the entryway, wiping her hands on a towel. "Petra told me to expect you," she said with a smile. "Welcome!"

Marlys nodded at the children. "I see you have company."

Hilde smiled and set the towel over a shoulder. "Yes, their parents, Nora and Leith, come regularly, bring supplies from the nearby village, and help me with repairs. We were fixing kitchen cabinets and I told the children to answer the door. Hope you don't mind."

"Not at all," Marlys said.

Hilde turned to the children. "You can go back to what you were doing."

The children turned and ran off.

"What were they doing, if I may ask?" Rochelle said.

"Exploring the fortress. They have favorite rooms," Hilde said.

"They must know the fortress fairly well," Marlys said.

"Almost as well as I do." Hilde gestured. "I'll show you to your rooms."

"Do they ever get lost?" Tir asked as they walked along.

"I modified the locator spell," Hilde said. "I can tell where they are at any time, and they know it."

"Must make playing hide-and-seek a dull exercise," Tir said.

Hilde smiled. "I don't participate, so they're free to find each other."

"The spell's already cast, I presume?" Marlys said.

"Long ago," Hilde replied. "Your presence won't affect it."

"Can you teach it to us, even though we can't cast it here ourselves?" Marlys said.

"I'd be happy to," Hilde said.

After Hilde showed them their rooms, and after they set down their traveling packs, Hilde escorted them to the fortress library. "I presume you want to read the spell books?"

"Yes, we do," Marlys said.

"They're on the shelves." Hilde gestured. "I need to go back and help with the kitchen repairs. I'll send the children up with food and drink. They were excited when I said there were other sorcerers coming. I'm the only one they've ever seen."

After Hilde had gone, Serena said, "Spell books. Plural."

Tir examined the shelves. "Yes, I think I've found them."

Marlys stepped next to him. "Just two. Serena can take one and I'll take the other."

Tir turned to Rochelle. "That leaves the journals and histories for us."

There were two tables in the room. Serena and Marlys sat across from each other at one table. Tir and Rochelle sat across from each other at the other.

Not too long afterwards, the three children entered, each with a tray. One had a tray with plates and small cakes. Another carried a tray with cups and saucers. The tallest one carried a tray with a teapot and a box of tea. They set them on the tables.

"Thank you," Marlys said. She and the other sorcerers helped themselves and sat again. When the children lingered, Marlys added. "There seem to be plenty of cakes. Go ahead and take one if you wish."

They did.

"What are your names?" Marlys asked.

The tallest one, a boy, pointed to himself. "I'm Lind. That's my sister Gaea and my brother Pen."

Marlys introduced herself and the others, then went back to reading.

The children remained but separated. Gaea stood next to Serena's shoulder as she read. Serena briefly turned and smiled at the child, then went back to reading. After a few minutes of watching Serena turn the pages, she said, "You read fast."

Serena faced Gaea. "I am a fast reader. I can read even faster if I use my special spell, but I can't use it here."

Pen, who stood next to Tir watching him read, said, "That's because of the orbs. The sorcerers used to be mean to each other. The orbs stop that."

Marlys nodded. "Did Hilde tell you that?"

Pen shook his head. "It's in the books."

Serena said, "Have you read the books?"

"We've read all of them," Lind said.

"Do you understand what they say?" Rochelle asked.

"Mostly," Lind said. "The spell books are the hardest. We aren't sure what the spells all mean. We've tried to do what the book says, but nothing happens."

Marlys smiled. "You'd have to be sorcerers yourselves to make things happen."

"That's what Hilde told us," Gaea said.

"But we play sorcerers anyway," Pen said.

"Hilde shows us real spells sometimes," Lind said. "She can do a lot."

"I'm sure she can," Marlys said.

Pen turned to Tir. "There's a story about a boy sorcerer in that book."

"There is?" Tir said.

Pen grabbed the book and turned the pages. "It's right here." He placed his finger on a page, then pushed the book back to Tir.

"Thank you," Tir said. "I'd be interested in reading that."

"Are you trying to find out how to cast spells?" Gaea asked Serena.

"We're looking to see if the books have any spells we don't know yet. Sorcerers are taught most of the same spells everywhere."

"What if you can't find anything new in the book?" Gaea asked.

"We also will explore the castle to see what we can find," Marlys said. "Sometimes in the old days, sorcerers would hide things to keep them safe or secret."

"We can help with that!" Lind said. "We've been all around the castle here."

"We know lots of hiding places," Gaea added.

Marlys stood, leaving the book she was reading open in front of her. "Show us."

The children ran out.

Serena stood. "We can read the books later. The children will probably only be here a while longer, until the repairs are done."

"I'm all for it," Rochelle said, getting out of her chair.

Tir slid his chair back. "I'm ready for a tour."

The children lingered in the hallway, waiting for the sorcerers to catch up. Then they hurried down the hallway. The adults rushed after them.

Lind stopped at a spot where sconces had been fastened to the walls. The candles there were currently unlit. "This is the best place."

Rochelle looked around. "It's well hidden. I don't see anything."

"You have to pull the candle holders," Pen said. "We're not supposed to, because we might break them."

Marlys exchanged a knowing look with the others. The children had probably pulled on them anyway.

Rochelle pulled a sconce. They heard a click. Lind pushed at the wall, and a section turned inward, as if it were a door. The inside was dark. They could see only a little with the lights from nearby windows. Tir lit a candle using household magic and lifted it out of the sconce. The children remained in the hall while the sorcerers went inside.

The room was about the size of a large closet. Marlys noted no dusty odor and saw no dust. The only object in the room was a large wooden chest. It had a latch but no lock.

Rochelle turned to Serena. "Should we open it?"

"It's all right," Lind said. "Nothing will happen."

"Have you seen what's inside?" Marlys asked.

"Keys," Gaea said. "But they don't fit anything here."

Rochelle opened the chest. They saw several keys. Rochelle took one out. In contrast to the key they found at Castlemount, this one was about as large as Marlys's hand. It was not wooden or metal, but some sort of ceramic. The handle had an ornate design of circular swirls. The rest of the key was shaped like a traditional key, straight on one side with several indentations on the other.

Serena reached in and took another key. "They seem to be identical." She held the key next to the one in Rochelle's hand to study the difference. "Yes, identical."

Tir took another one out. "You're right, all identical."

Marlys turned to the children. "What did Hilde say about this?"

The children put their hands behind their backs and swayed a little from side to side.

"Ah, I see," Marlys said. "You didn't tell Hilde."

"We didn't want to get in trouble," Pen said.

"But you showed us," Tir said.

When the children again did not answer, Marlys turned to him. "I think the responsibility has been transferred to us." She leaned toward the children. "Don't worry, we'll keep your secret."

The children let out sighs of relief.

"Sure," Rochelle said. "We can tell Hilde we found it, which we did."

Serena put the key she was holding back in the chest. "I think we only need one. Rochelle, can you hold on to that one?"

"Of course."

Tir put his key back and latched the chest again. The sorcerers all stepped out in the hall.

"How do you close this thing?" Rochelle said. "There aren't any handles."

"Pull the candle holder again," Lind said.

Tir snuffed out the candle, replaced it in the holder, and pulled the holder. The door slid back into place.

Marlys felt the wall. "Hardly even a seam to tell it was there." She turned to the children. "Are there any other hiding places? We won't tell anyone what you show us if you don't want us to."

The children hurried away again. They showed the sorcerers numerous panels and cubbyholes, especially in the stone walls of the lowest levels. However, the slips of paper recorded spells already known to them, and the artifacts found were keepsakes common to sorcerers: ribbons commemorating the first performance of a difficult spell, badges or trinkets given upon attaining sorcerous powers, and so forth.

Lastly, the children escorted them to the orb room.

"We like to sit here and talk to the orbs," Lind said.

"What do they say to you?" Rochelle asked.

"They don't use words," Gaea said, "but we talk to them, and we feel happy."

"That's good," Marlys said.

"There's nothing else here, we just wanted to show them to you," Lind said.

"They're always worth the visit," Tir said.

Rochelle held up the key. "The key seems to think so. It's reverberating."

"It is?" Tir said.

Rochelle brought the key closer to the orbs.

"Looks as if it's glowing," Marlys said.

"Faintly, yes," Rochelle said.

"Talking to each other?" Tir said.

They all remained quiet for a few minutes while the key and orbs brightened and dimmed together.

"They're happy," Gaea said.

"If we separate them again, will either become unhappy?" Tir asked.

"We can't stay here forever," Marlys said.

"I'll back away slowly," Rochelle said.

Rochelle edged her way toward the stairs. The key's glow slowly went away. The orbs returned to their steady glow.

Marlys let out a breath. "I think we're fine. Let's get back to the library."

As they walked back through the hallways, they heard Leith and Nora calling to the children. The sorcerers, including Hilde, walked to the front door with the family. Leith and Nora had packed up the tools and placed them in a horse-drawn wagon. They lifted the children into the wagon and sat in the front to take the reins. They all waved at each other as the wagon rolled away.

When they were gone, Hilde closed the front door.

"We have something to show you," Marlys said.

They all sat in the dining area. Rochelle had placed the key on the table. Hilde picked it up and examined it. "Where did you find this?"

"There's a secret closet at the library level," Marlys said.

Hilde turned to Marlys. "You must be good at finding things. I had no idea there was a secret closet and the book for the hosts here at Hilltop has no mention of it."

"We're always stumbling into things at our own fortress," Marlys said. "The sorcerers of old were famous for keeping their favorite spells to themselves."

"And hiding things anywhere and everywhere," Serena added.

"That's for certain," Hilde said. "There's a lot of that in the old books. I find things here all the time I didn't know about. I'm glad that we're more open about sharing knowledge now." She gestured around the room. "That's what the Spell Passage is for, in the end, saving and sharing knowledge."

Serena reached out and touched the key. "Do you have any idea what this might be? We've been all through this castle, and there's no lock we saw that this would fit."

"I haven't seen a lock that size, either," Hilde said. "Unless there's some hidden keyhole somewhere."

"We found this in a chest in the closet with several identical keys," Tir said. "That seems to imply an intent to distribute."

"Yes, but where?" Hilde said.

"At this point, we don't know," Marlys said. "Do you mind if we take this with us? When we eventually get back to Goldenvalley, we can study it and send word with what we find."

"Yes, take it. Once you're gone, I'll talk with the other station hosts through the sorcerous channels to see what they think."

"One thing more," Rochelle said. "The orbs seem to respond to it."

"Now that's interesting," Hilde said.

"It was a gentle encounter," Rochelle said. "Reminded me of two musicians playing the same tune."

Tir turned to her. "Yes, that's what it reminded me of, too."

"In the meantime," Marlys said, "we need to get back to the library and continue reading the spell books."

When they gathered for dinner, Hilde asked, "Did you find the spells you were looking for?"

Serena shook her head. "Nothing new to us, no."

Tir grinned. "I found that there used to be a legendary sorcerer named Elias. He, and I say again, he, was a notable scholar. He started the first spell libraries and it is said that he collected the knowledge of the time into the Library of Sorcery."

"Yes, I remember reading about him," Hilde said. "Well-spoken. Charming. Good looking."

Rochelle turned to Tir. "Reminds me of someone I know."

Tir smiled.

Marlys winked at him.

Serena nodded in Tir's direction and turned to Hilde. "Before we go, we still want to learn your version of the locator spell."

"I'll be happy to show you before you leave," Hilde said. "It's not hard. In return, don't forget to show me where you found the keys."

"We will," Marlys said.

Chapter 16

The next day, they made their way to the Overlook fortress. When they stepped out of the distance shortening spell, they saw the fortress nearby. Another edifice, immediately to their left, drew their attention.

Tir looked up. "A freestanding tower?"

"Does that recess near the top look like a window to you?" Rochelle said. "Looks like a door to me."

"With a ledge," Serena added.

"I'm going to walk around and see if there's an entrance at this level," Tir said.

The others followed.

When they made a complete circuit, Marlys said, "It's a typical tower. Square cross-section, stone-and-mortar walls, conical copper roof. But no opening at the ground."

Rochelle craned her neck to see the top. "I suppose one could use a grappling hook tied to a rope."

"And use sorcery to get the hook up there," Serena said.

Rochelle turned to Marlys. "But what would you put there, and would it be worth the trouble to get it there?"

Marlys shrugged. "I don't know. Perhaps we could ask our host."

Tir kindled a sorcerous light. "We are out of range of the sorcery-nullifying spell here."

"I wonder where the dividing point is," Rochelle said.

"We can find out." Tir extinguished the light, walked five paces, and kindled it again successfully. He turned it off, walked another five paces, and conjured the light again. After the next five paces, he tried the spell once more, but this time there was no result.

He turned. "The dividing point is here."

Marlys nodded. "That's useful to know. For now, let's continue on to the fortress."

They proceeded to the front steps and rang the bell. The door swung open, revealing a sturdy young woman wearing a necklace of small, iridescent seashells.

She smiled. "I'm Kayli. Hilde told me to expect you. Welcome." She gestured. "Come in."

After they assembled in the hallway, Kayli closed the door. Marlys made the introductions.

Rochelle indicated the necklace. "Are you from the Oceanside region?"

She nodded. "Yes. Challengers Cove."

"Safe Harbor," Rochelle said. "Just south of you."

"Right in the neighborhood," Kayli said. "Here, let me show you where to stow your packs. Then we can sit and talk."

Later, the four of them settled in the main reception room. A fire blazed in the fireplace. Tea, muffins, butter, and jam had been set on a low table between two long couches.

"What brings you so far from home?" Rochelle asked.

"Many have said that the sea is relaxing, refreshing," Kayli said. "It can be that for some. But I had a yearning for hills and mountains."

Rochelle took a bite of buttered muffin, chewed, and swallowed. "There are cliffs at Safe Harbor."

Kayli nodded. "I have seen them. But the sea is ever raging, and the mountains here, away from the ocean, are quiet in comparison."

"Is there something about these particular mountains?" Marlys said. "Mountain ranges closer to the ocean can be found elsewhere in the continent."

Kayli settled back into the couch. "True. But most of the sorcerers in this area came to this place seeking independence, a place to develop our skills outside a more structured system… not to fault yours," she added with a nod toward Marlys.

"I understand," Marlys said. "Our system is not for everyone."

"Of course," Kayli continued. "Here we are a smaller group. We all know each other, we train each other, share our spell knowledge. We're happy here."

"That's good," Marlys said. "It makes for better sorcery when everyone's satisfied with the way it is practiced."

Rochelle refilled her teacup from the teapot. "When I left Safe Harbor to find a place that would train me as a sorcerer, the elder sorcerer at the trainer facility told me that if I didn't feel I fit in, I could go and find another place to learn and no one would think ill of me for it. My fellow apprentices were nice enough, but I wanted something else. That's what brought me to Goldenvalley."

"How many sorcerers here are from elsewhere, and how many grew up here?" Serena asked.

"Most came from outside. That's good because the population in this area isn't large enough to produce many sorcerers. I know Gweneth over at Stronghold was born in this area," Kayli said. "I think Brianna at Wishborne, your next stop, and I have traveled the farthest. Brianna is from Majesticacres."

"How does everyone find their way here?" Marlys said. "The sorcerers all know where to find the Spell Passage, but people growing up outside the area might not."

"We send ambassadors with the merchants that travel from the mining and smelting areas to the outlying towns," Kayli said.

"Not the groups of merchants that go through the central regions, I presume," Marlys said.

Kayli nodded. "The ambassadors have a good reputation. When they encounter those who can do household spells, they talk about this area and invite them to think about becoming sorcerers. We even have a few notable sorcerers in the vicinity.""

"Notable?" Rochelle asked.

Kayli gestured toward Tir. "Like Tir, here."

"Another man?" Tir asked eagerly.

"Yes, but different. I can tell that you, Tir, have transitioned. I hope you don't mind my mentioning it."

"Not at all," Tir said.

"In this case, there was no transition. Durand was assigned as male at birth and could do household spells from childhood."

"That's extraordinary," Marlys said.

"Even more," Kayli said, "he was the son of a sorcerer."

"I have never heard of a sorcerer giving birth, ever," Rochelle said. "Serena, have you ever heard or read of this?"

Serena shook her head. "Never."

"Where is Durand now?" Tir asked.

"He is one of the senior sorcerers at our training center near the iron mines," Kayli said, "but as soon as you left Stronghold, Gweneth contacted him through the sorcerous channels."

"He's a sorcerer?" Tir asked.

"He is," Kayli said. "He's on his way here. He was hoping to meet you."

"And I him!" Tir said.

"Any other notables?" Rochelle asked.

"Two," Kayli said. "Lumina, the sorcerer at the last stop on the Passage, was assigned as male at birth, but she felt she was destined to be a sorcerer."

"She could do household spells, I presume," Rochelle asked.

Kayli nodded. "Her family dismissed them as imagination or tricks at first, but our ambassador told her that if she wanted to be a sorcerer, she should come to our training center when she was of age."

"You said two?" Serena said.

"Nolor, a sorcerer residing at one of the towns near the Passage, retired, but still using sorcery when needed, is neither gender."

"The Bright Beings are ever bestowing their gifts," Marlys said.

From the reception room, Marlys and her companions went to the library to read the books. They had not been there long when they heard the bell for the front door. The door to the library was open, and the sound carried.

"Durand!" Kayli's voice came.

"Sorry I'm later than expected," said a booming male voice. "We had some heavy rains lately, and I had to do some flood control with the Rushing River."

"We all need to attend to our sorcerous duties first," Kayli said. "Besides, you're right on time. They're here. Can I take your cloak and pack?"

"Yes, thank you," Durand said. "Then I want to see your visitors."

"Of course."

They heard footsteps treading the stairs. Soon Kayli and Durand came into the library. Durand was sturdily built, with a short beard. Both beard and hair had gray streaks.

Durand spread his arms. "Welcome, brother and sisters! It's been a long time since sorcerers from the regions have attempted the Passage." He stepped in Tir's direction. Tir rose and walked over. The two men embraced in a bear hug.

When he released Tir, Durand said, "I thought I'd never see another man in the practice of sorcery."

"Nor I," said Tir.

Durand turned to the others. "You must be Marlys, Serena, and Rochelle. I'm Durand."

The others waved as he spoke their names to identify themselves.

"Can you spare Tir for a time so we can speak together?"

"If that's what Tir wants to do, yes," Marlys said.

"I'll try not to be gone too long," Tir said.

"Take your time," Marlys said.

"We'll be in the room with the glowing rocks, if you need us," Durand said.

The two men left.

"I'll start dinner," Kayli said.

"Need help?" Rochelle asked.

"No, but thank you for your offer." She walked out.

The room remained silent for a while.

Eventually, Serena lifted her head. "I think I've found a spell we don't know."

Marlys and Rochelle put their books down and gathered behind her.

"A climbing spell?" Rochelle said.

"Could be," Serena said.

"Probably useful for getting into the tower we saw," Marlys said.

"I used to climb the cliffs back home," Rochelle said. "Let's try it."

"I'm willing," Serena said.

"Bring the book," Marlys said.

They stopped in the underground rooms where Tir and Durand sat side-by-side.

Marlys ducked in. "We're going outside to try out the climbing spell we found."

"You haven't tried it?" Durand said.

"No, we hadn't heard of it before," Marlys said.

Durand stood. "We were done here anyway and about to find you." He put a hand on Tir's shoulder. "You have to try it. It's fun."

Tir stood. "Let's go."

Once outside, they gathered at the base of the tower.

"We test the sorcerers here with this spell once they've come into their powers," Durand said. "It's sort of a rite of passage."

"We use spells to push and pull, but they're not very accurate pushing or pulling something up or down," Marlys said.

"And it's possible for the object being pushed or pulled to slip," Serena added.

Rochelle put her hand against the tower's surface. "I used to be able to put a hand or foot on the slightest protrusion without using sorcery, but this is just too smooth."

"There's a legend that it was put here by the Bright Beings," Durand said. "But no one knows for sure. It's very old, older than the fortress."

"What's up there?" Tir asked.

"Sorcerous objects of ancient origin," Durand said, "such as the singing crystals you saw at Heathervale." As the others craned their necks, he added, "I'll go first, and open the door."

"Good," Rochelle said. "We'll watch you perform the spell."

Durand stepped closer to the tower wall. He lowered his head briefly, gathering his thoughts. Then he made the appropriate gestures and began to climb, as if an invisible ladder had appeared. When he reached the ledge, he pulled himself up, opened the door, and looked down. "Who's next?"

"I'll go." Marlys leaned over to read the book again, open in Serena's hands, to review the instructions. She stepped to the wall, put herself in the correct frame of mind, gestured as Durand did, and put up a hand. She saw nothing but felt something, as if the air had stiffened, to put her hand on. When she pulled up and raised a foot, her foot met something to step on. Slowly, she climbed, gaining more speed and confidence as she went. When she drew even with the ledge, Durand put out a hand and helped her up and in.

Marlys looked down. "Easier than I thought. Try it."

The others followed without incident. Serena cast a spell to secure the spell book against the side of the wall before ascending.

Tir kindled a sorcerous light and stepped into the room. A round table graced the middle of the room. A large, elegantly-bound book lay open there. The wall had many alcoves, housing various objects.

Serena walked directly to the book, sparking a sorcerous light of her own. "Very old style writing, but the book is in excellent condition."

Rochelle stepped next to Serena and looked down. "'Use only in need. Use wisely,'" she read.

Durand nodded. "No one knows for certain who wrote or left the book, or the artifacts." He gestured around. "You can't even touch the weapons on the wall: the knives, the swords. Some sort of protective spell."

"My guess would be that this is to prevent another sorcerous war," Marlys said.

"Agreed," Durand said. "The legend passed down among sorcerers here says that these are shielded until and unless a great need arises."

"Who can define that?" Serena asked.

"I have a feeling that if it arose, we would know without a doubt," Tir said.

Rochelle looked at other alcoves. "Not all of these are weapons."

"That's true." Durand walked to an alcove and touched what seemed to be a small, framed glass rectangle. "This is a nice trifle. It reflects your mood."

Serena walked over. "How so?"

Durand spoke to the glass. "Hello."

The surface of the glass formed an image of Durand's head and smiled. "Hello."

"Mimics your voice well," Tir said.

Durand turned to him. "Yes. Though if I were sad, and trying to cover it up, the sphere would show a sad expression and the voice would be sad."

"Dinner's ready." Kayli's voice called from outside.

Marlys went to the door and looked down. Kayli held the spell book as she looked up.

"How do we get down?" Rochelle asked.

"Same way you got up," Durand said.

Marlys cast the spell, backed to the edge of the ledge, and put a foot down. Feeling a solid support, she continued until she reached the ground.

The others followed. Durand closed the door and reached the ground last.

"Thank you," Marlys said. "It's always good to know a new spell."

"I would have thought that you would know it, too," Kayli said. "Though it has been years, others have come through and read the spell books."

"Somehow it never reached us," Marlys said.

"I hadn't heard of it," Serena said, "and I've read spell books throughout our regions."

"Spells get lost, spells get found," Durand said. "That's why it's good to stay connected."

"Once we reach home again," Marlys said, "I'll be sure we do."

Chapter 17

The dinner table featured platters of roast chicken and buttered bread among assorted fruits and vegetables. Kayli sat at the head of the table. Durand and Tir sat side-by-side at Kayli's right, while Marlys, Serena, and Rochelle sat at her left.

"You must tell us about your family," Marlys said, spearing a slice of chicken with the serving fork and passing the plate on to Serena.

"After she became a sorcerer, my mother settled in a town south of here to help others with her spells. A carpenter caught her eye, and they began spending time together. Eventually, they married."

"Unusual," Marlys said. "In my region, we've only started marrying sorcerers recently, though few express interest in marriage. Most remain uninterested in having sexual relations."

Durand nodded. "So it has been for millennia. Most people take that for granted, but occasionally a lass or lad has caught my eye with an invitation. I have had to politely say that while I know that many would appreciate the offer, it's simply not something I would wish to respond to."

"Thorne, who was high sorceress before me," Marlys said, "put a spell on the sorcerers in our region to enforce celibacy."

Durand laughed out loud. "Truly? Why work a spell when the Universe creates the condition naturally among sorcerers?"

"She never told me the reason," Marlys said. "I knew from a young age that coupling was not for me."

"I've always known it," Rochelle said.

Serena nodded in agreement.

Tir shrugged.

"Even married," Marlys continued, "we have yet to see a birth among sorcerers, however."

Durand nodded. "My parents noted the same. But they wanted a child. My mother thought that since there is sorcery that can aid fertility, why not try it on herself? I was the result."

"I wonder if the sorcerous conception had to do with your ability to do household spells," Serena said.

"We—my family—have always wondered," Durand said. "But it's only a guess. We don't know for sure."

"Among those we have used sorcery to help with conception," Marlys said, "there haven't been any more births of children who can do household spells than usual."

"Meaning that children who can do household spells are still rare," Serena said.

Durand nodded. "That's why it's still only a guess."

"No siblings?" Rochelle asked.

Durand smiled. "My mother said one pregnancy was enough."

Serena turned to Marlys. "Pregnancy among married sorcerers is something that's worth watching for when we return home."

Marlys nodded.

After dinner, they all helped clean up. Kayli and Durand gave them a tour of the fortress, but Marlys did not see anything unique that might help them in their quest. The tower, apparently, contained the learning that this step in the Passage had to give.

When they reached the visitors' rooms, Kayli said, "Will you be leaving tomorrow?"

"Yes," Marlys said. "Nothing to do with your hospitality, which is excellent. As we told you at dinner, we have obligations to attend to at home."

Kayli nodded. "I understand."

"Would you mind if I accompanied you to Wishborne?" Durand said. "I haven't been there for some time."

"By all means, join us," Marlys said.

Kayli smiled wryly. "Leaving me to face the following sorcerer and apprentice alone, Durand?"

"You're more than competent to handle them," Durand said.

Kayli noted the facial expressions on Marlys, Tir, Serena, and Rochelle. "I understand why you prefer not to discuss them. But the rest of us on the Passage have been making frequent use of the sorcerous channels."

"Trouble?" Marlys ventured cautiously.

"More of a nuisance," Kayli said. "Nothing we can't cope with, but we've found them incredibly naïve and unprepared."

Marlys, Serena, Rochelle, and Tir exchanged knowing looks. "Until breakfast, then," Kayli said.

The next day, Durand joined Marlys, Serena, Rochelle, and Tir as they gathered at the front door. They descended the stairs and waved to Kayli as she stood in the doorway, waving back.

Marlys turned to Durand, "Do you wish to do the honors and lead the way to Wishborne?"

Durand smiled. "I'd be happy to." He cast the spell to shorten the distance and they were on their way.

Brianna opened the door before any of them had a chance to pull the cord for the bell. She stood taller than any of them, with a glorious crown of black hair like Serena's.

"Durand," she said with a smile, "it's been too long since I've seen you in the flesh."

"Yes," he agreed. "Sorcerous channels are well and good, but face-to-face meetings are even better."

Brianna nodded at Marlys. "You must be Marlys. The others have described you. Welcome." She nodded at the remainder of the company, in turn. "Welcome, Serena. Welcome, Rochelle. Welcome, Tir. Come inside and let me show you to your rooms. Then we can sit and talk."

When they had settled into the chairs and couches of the reception room, Brianna set down a plate at the table. The dish held round yellow and pink discs.

Rochelle reached for one. "Candies?"

Brianna sat and nodded. "I make my own."

Rochelle bit one, chewed, swallowed, and waved a hand in appreciation. "Mm. Delicious. Best I've ever tasted." She turned to the others. "Try one."

The others did, and extended their compliments as well.

After Durand ate one, he turned to Brianna. "Everyone along the Passage is a good to great cook, but Brianna is a level above."

When they finished the tea and candies, Brianna showed the way to the library.

"If you don't mind," Durand said, "I'll go to the kitchen with Brianna and catch up."

"By all means," Marlys said.

Durand put a hand on Tir's shoulder. Tir smiled and nodded. Durand followed Brianna out.

After a time, Marlys closed the book she had been reading. "As we've gone along, I've noticed that the books have essentially the same information at each step in the Passage."

Rochelle closed the book in front of her. "I've noticed it, too."

Tir closed his book. "Nothing new here."

Serena turned pages in the spell book. "I have been skimming unless I find something that looks new. Wait." She flipped some pages ahead and then flipped back.

"Something?" Marlys said.

Serena frowned. "Yes, this is a spell book. Everything we already know, except...," She looked up. "What's a recipe doing in a spell book?"

The others gathered around and looked over her shoulder.

"Turn those pages back," Marlys said, "and then forward again."

Serena obliged, then turned to Marlys.

Tir scratched his head. "I know little about cooking, but that certainly looks like a recipe to me."

"Me, too," Rochelle chimed in.

"Time to consult our host?" Tir asked.

"Let's give it a little more study first." Marlys drew a chair up next to Serena and sat.

Tir and Rochelle did the same.

Serena kept the book open so that they all could read it.

Marlys tapped a place on the page. "A recipe with a difference."

"I see it," Serena said.

"Could this be true?" Rochelle said. "Imbue the ingredients with sorcery?"

"Seems so," Marlys said.

"I've been preserving food with household magic since I was a child," Tir said. "But this is different."

"But what would sorcery add?" Rochelle said. "Sorcery can't create food. It can preserve food, cook food, freeze food."

"Let's keep reading," Serena said. "Tell me when you have read to the bottom of the page, and I'll turn it."

After the next page, recording of various spells resumed.

Serena scanned the following pages. "No new spells to the end." She turned back to the recipe page.

Marlys pushed her chair back a little. "If I'm reading this correctly, this recipe, once made, will keep forever."

Serena nodded. "And, one can survive well on this and water alone."

"Better than simply bread and water, or even bread and tubers," Marlys added.

Rochelle leaned over. "Not only survive, but thrive, giving the eater strength and endurance."

"I wonder how it tastes," Tir said.

"Common ingredients," Marlys said. "Most are the same ingredients we use to make bread, cakes, muffins, and other tasty treats."

"Local flavorings, though," Serena said, "I haven't seen them anywhere else."

"I haven't, either," Marlys said. "Now is the time we consult our host, I think,"

Serena took the book and they all made their way to the kitchen, where Brianna and Durand stood side-by-side at a counter.

"Dinner's almost ready," Brianna said.

"Everything looks good," Tir said.

"We found a recipe in the spell book," Serena said.

Brianna nodded. "Good. Set the book at the end of the table in the dining room and we'll discuss it over supper."

Supper consisted of a hearty stew of meat and vegetables. Bread and fruit had been placed on the table, along with a teapot and a pitcher of milk.

"I gather you found the recipe for the waycake." Durand poured milk into a mug.

"Is that what it's called?" Tir said as he reached for a bread roll and the tub of butter.

"That's what we call it," Brianna said. "The recipe was discovered in one of the underground rooms centuries ago, folded in a long narrow box placed in a crack in the wall."

"Whoever placed the recipe there must have thought it important," Marlys said, "if they made an effort to preserve the paper."

"We send the waycakes with our ambassadors when they go out," Brianna said, "in case they find themselves in a barren land with no food."

"They're delicious, too," Durand said.

"Do you have any ready made that we can try?" Tir asked.

Brianna shook her head slightly. "No, we only make waycakes at need. The flavoring is from a plant that only grows here."

"I've tried to find it in my travels with no success," Durand added.

Brianna reached for her cup of tea. "We've also tried to grow it elsewhere. It just—won't."

"Can you show us the plant in case we see it?" Serena asked.

"Of course," Brianna said. "There's a patch in our garden in back of the fortress."

"We're planning to go to the Library of Sorcery," Marlys said. "Can you show us how to prepare waycakes to bring with us? We understand the area along the way has little to offer in the way of food."

Brianna nodded. "That's what we're here for. It would be better if you watch me make them and assist when needed. I had to watch my predecessor here put the recipe together twice before I was able to do it alone. However, I can't show you how to use sorcery to fortify the ingredients. That I do when there aren't other sorcerers here. You'll need to remember the technique from the spell book."

"It's a complicated procedure, even using ingredients already fortified," Durand added. "I've watched her do it more than twice and I can't do it,"

"It seems that whoever originated this recipe wanted to be sure that it was not lost, but not commonly used if found," Serena observed.

"That is our guess," Brianna said.

After breakfast the next day, Brianna led the other sorcerers outside to the garden and pointed out the flavoring plant. She showed how to harvest it so that the roots remained intact and the plant would grow again.

Back in the kitchen, the others gathered ingredients at Brianna's direction. Marlys and Serena, who were the most experienced cooks, watched Brianna closely and assisted when asked. Durand directed Tir and Rochelle in sorting and wrapping the waycakes as they were finished.

Brianna made two extra waycakes, cutting each into small pieces so that everyone could have a taste.

Tir nibbled on his, as if to make it last as long as possible, and then licked the crumbs from his fingers. "You were right, Durand. This is good."

"You only need one waycake every day," Brianna said, "so use them sparingly."

"We will," Marlys said. "Thank you."

Chapter 18

Durand asked if he could go to the Pinnacle fortress with them, the final stop on the Spell Passage. When they all arrived at the front door, they heard a voice.

"Welcome to Pinnacle!"

They turned to see a woman walking toward them. The handle of a basket of flowers was slung over an arm.

Durand walked up to her. "Good to see you, Lumina." He embraced her carefully, avoiding disturbing the basket.

When he stepped back, Lumina said, "Good to see you, too, Durand." She looked around him. "You must be Marlys, Serena, Rochelle, and Tir."

"We are," Marlys affirmed.

"I went out to gather flowers before you came," Lumina said. "Sorcery preserves flowers so much better than household spells."

Rochelle pointed over her shoulder. "Do you need us to go back for a bit so you can use sorcery?"

"No," Lumina said cheerfully. "They're already preserved. I did it as soon as I picked them." She waved a hand at the door. "Come inside." She led the way up the stairs to the door. With her free hand, she reached into a pocket of her brightly patterned smock and took out a large key.

"Will that fit the keyhole?" Tir asked.

"I just need to touch the lock with this," Lumina explained. "It's a long-established spell. The key is just shaped that way to remind me what it does."

"Do you always lock your doors in this remote place?" Rochelle asked as Durand pushed the door open for Lumina and the others to go through.

When they had assembled in the entryway, Lumina said, "Much of the time there are no visitors at all. But it would only take one person to slip inside to remove artifacts. My predecessor said that the stations on the Spell Passage were too important to take chances." She placed the basket on a small table. "Come. Let me show you to your rooms and then we can gather and talk."

When they were settled in the reception room, with tea and cakes on the table next to a large vase holding flowers, Lumina said to Tir, "I see that you have transitioned, too."

Tir nodded and took a sip of tea. "Yes, I have. Couldn't be happier."

"As am I," Lumina said. "In the town where I grew up, everybody knew somebody whose distant cousin, or grandfather's best friend, went to a sorcerer to remake their body and complete their transition. They said I should do that, too. But I could also do household spells. I decided that I didn't just want a sorcerer to help me with my transition, I wanted to be a sorcerer when I was old enough. When I reached that age, I was taken in as an apprentice."

"It happened to be the same place where I was trained as a sorcerer," Durand said.

"There seems to be somewhere for everybody," Rochelle said.

Lumina nodded. "Being a Passage host suited me, too. When I learned about the Spell Passage as an apprentice, I knew right away that this is where I wanted to be."

"Yes, it's a lovely place," Serena said. "Besides the flowers, I was admiring the bedspreads, the pillowcases, and the curtains."

"Not to mention the embroidery," Marlys said.

"I sew," Lumina said. "I have a lot of time for it here."

"She does more than sewing," Durand said.

"Yes. I stamp the coins I will give you for completing the Spell Passage," Lumina said.

"Do you design those?" Tir asked.

Lumina shook her head. "No, the design's been the same for centuries."

"Tradition," Durand said.

Lumina turned to Marlys and her companions. "You'll have something to take home with you to show your friends. You're welcome to stay as long as you wish, of course, within reason. I'm not hurrying you."

"We do want to read your spell books," Serena said.

"And explore the fortress," Tir added.

"You are more than welcome to do that," Lumina said.

"We'll stay a couple of days at least," Marlys said. "But then we need to be off to find the Library of Sorcery."

Lumina nodded. "The other hosts mentioned to me through the sorcerous channels that you wanted to do that. It's a serious undertaking. No one else except a party of three from Woodlands has tried it since I have been the host at Pinnacle. They returned saying that they weren't able to reach it."

"Nonetheless, we're determined to try," Marlys said.

Lumina put her teacup back on the table. "Then I'll be outfitting you, too. You'll need all the aid that we can offer."

"We will be glad for that," Marlys said.

Lumina showed them the way to the fortress's library. After familiarizing the newcomers with the room's contents, she and Durand left them to page through the spell books. They browsed through those and quickly surmised that they contained little they had not seen before.

After leaving the library, they set out to explore the fortress. Everywhere they saw flower arrangements, beautifully preserved. Curtains adorned windows. Embroidered cloths covered tables. But room after room held nothing of sorcerous interest.

They found Lumina and Durand in a large room on the lower levels. The two sorted through clothing on a table. More clothing, mostly coats and jackets, hung on racks near the walls. Gloves, scarves, cloaks, socks, and other accessories lay neatly folded on upper shelves. Sturdy shoes and boots of various sizes were neatly arranged on lower shelves.

Lumina looked up. "You found us. Good. We pulled out items that we thought would suit you, but it's better that you try them on than for us to guess whether they would fit."

Marlys placed a hand on a coat's sleeve. "We wouldn't need much, I think. We brought clothes with us, and we keep them and ourselves clean with household spells."

"True," Lumina said, "but household spells won't keep you comfortable on hard and rough terrain when you're ready to sleep."

"We could spread our coats on the ground and sleep on those," Rochelle said.

"The foothills of the Mountains of Wrath are rugged beyond what you have in the regions," Durand said. "I know. I've been an ambassador and have traveled the length and width of the continent."

"To the Library of Sorcery?" Tir asked.

Durand smiled. "No, not that far. But yes, in sight of the Shadowmount. Just to say I've seen it." He held up a hand and pointed at a cabinet next to a wall. "Bedrolls. That's what you need." He walked to the cabinet and opened it. Reaching in, he took out a roll of tightly-woven gray fabric.

The others followed.

Marlys felt the fabric. "Seems a little thin for a bedroll."

"It's spelled," Durand explained. "When spread out, the stuffing will expand and the lining will thicken. Much better to sleep on."

"We'll take it," Marlys said.

Meanwhile, Rochelle rummaged in the cabinet and pulled out a coil of thin rope. "I presume this is stronger than it looks?"

Lumina nodded. "Also spelled."

Rochelle smiled. "I'll take it, and a couple of grappling hooks as well."

Lumina nodded at Durand. "We need to start supper. Please go through the supplies and take what you think you need."

"The question is, what do you think we need?" Marlys said.

Durand gestured to the bedroll and the rope. "Beyond these, you probably have what is necessary. But if you want sturdier gloves or boots, or other supplies, just grab them."

"Thank you," Marlys said.

They spent some time sorting through all the items and determining what might be best to add to their packs. When finished, they each gathered what they had set aside, and went to their rooms, where they rearranged their baggage. Tir and Rochelle had each taken a larger pack. Marlys and Serena managed to stuff or attach what they had acquired in or onto their existing packs.

After they sat down for dinner, Lumina said, "I'll strike your coins this evening."

"I'd like to watch that," Tir said.

"Please do," Lumina said.

"Will you be leaving soon or lingering for a time?" Durand asked.

"We seem to have everything we need to begin our journey to the Mountains of Wrath," Marlys said, "but I want to wait for the party behind us to join us here first."

"Do you think they'd be willing to do that?" Rochelle asked.

"I think that since we're going to the same destination, and since it's going to be a difficult journey by all accounts, it's better for us to travel together than separately," Marlys said.

"Isn't the point for us to get there first?" Tir said.

"I thought so when we started out," Marlys said. "But as we've gathered information, it seems to me that sooner or later, we're bound to find ourselves on the same path, so we may as well go together."

"I'll repeat Tir's thought," Serena said. "Isn't the point for us to get there first?"

Marlys nodded. "I know what you mean, but even in the case where the information we want is there, and they find it first, we can still do what we need to do, and they can't prevent us from doing so."

After a few seconds of contemplative silence, Serena nodded. "I see what you're saying."

Rochelle turned to Marlys. "That isn't the main problem. Sure, we're willing to have them join us. The question is whether they will refuse to do so."

Again, silence. Everyone continued eating.

Eventually, Lumina held up a hand. "I sense there's some sort of dispute, and no, I don't want to know about it. But in discussions with the other hosts through the sorcerous channels, I understand that the party following you has shown signs of, shall I say, stubbornness?"

"That's the truth," Rochelle murmured.

"Perhaps I can offer my services," Durand said. "Earlier, I talked about the times when I was an ambassador in my younger days. Settling matters between groups was a regular event. I agree with Lumina that we aren't going to take sides in any disputes you may have. But, as an independent party, I may be able to convince the other team that cooperation is in their best interest."

"We would be grateful if you could," Marlys said. "You'll have to go back to Wishborne to talk to them, however, since I doubt that they will come here of their own accord if they realize we're here."

"Ah," Lumina said. "That solves a mystery. The other hosts have said that Nessa and Zaria have left their fortresses, seemingly to continue on their way, and then have unexpectedly returned."

"Yes," Serena said, "they would have to leave the fortress in order to cast the locator spell."

"Well, they won't be watching out for me," Durand said.

After dinner, Lumina led them to a room in the fortress with a table in the middle. On the table they saw a stack of blank, shiny, silvery disks, each about the size of a coin or large button. Next to the stack they saw a device with a die on both sides with a lever to bring the forms together. She placed a disk on the lower die, then pressed hard on the lever. Releasing the lever, she took the disk and presented it to Marlys.

"Your coin."

"Thank you." Marlys accepted the coin and examined it. It had been stamped on both sides with the image of an open book.

Lumina stamped three more coins and gave them to the others.

"One task that doesn't require sorcery," Durand observed.

"With the sentinel stones preventing sorcery, it would have to be done without the use of spells," Lumina observed.

Durand nodded and rubbed his hands together. "I'll be on my way then."

"So soon?" Tir asked.

"Yes, I've been away from home long enough. I'll stop at Wishborne then be on my way." He hugged Tir and slapped him on the back. "Good to meet you, brother."

"And you," Tir said.

Durand hugged Marlys, Serena, and Rochelle in turn. "Pleasure to meet you," he said to each of them, and each replied the same.

As Durand turned to go, Marlys said, "If you're ever in the vicinity of Goldenvalley, see us. You'll be welcome."

"If I'm ever in that vicinity, I will," Durand said.

Chapter 19

The next day, Marlys and the others were in the supply room when they heard voices at the front door.

"Welcome to Pinnacle," Lumina said cheerily.

Nessa replied, "Can we have quiet rooms away from everyone else?"

"Of course. There's plenty of room," Lumina said.

They heard three sets of footsteps proceeding down a hallway and up stairs.

Tir turned to Marlys. "Durand seems to have convinced them."

"Nessa sounds as sour as ever," Rochelle added.

"One step at a time," Marlys said.

At the midday meal, Nessa and Zaria sat on one side of the table. Marlys and her company sat on the other side. Lumina sat at the head.

Lumina turned to Nessa and Zaria. "After we eat, I can strike the coin you've earned for completing the spell passage."

Nessa put down her fork, which had just speared a slice of fruit. "What coin?"

In answer, Serena turned up her sleeve and showed hers, sewn to the hem. She held it up for them to see.

"It's very nice," Tir observed as he buttered a piece of bread.

Nessa turned to Lumina. "Are we obliged to take one?"

"No," Lumina said, still sounding upbeat. "You don't have to have one if you don't want one."

Zaria faced Nessa. "I want mine. A small reward, at least, for all the trouble we've been through."

Nessa sighed and forced a faint smile. "We'll be happy to take a coin, thank you."

Lumina nodded. "Are you planning to go to the Library of Sorcery, too?"

Zaria reached for the basket of bread rolls. "That was the point of this entire journey."

"Then you'll want to visit our supply room. You're welcome to take anything you wish."

Nessa finished chewing the slice of fruit and touched her lips with a napkin. "We have everything we need."

"No, you don't," Tir said. "Remember Stronghold?"

Nessa glared at him.

Tir chuckled. "Scowl all you want, but the terrain is rugged on the approach to Shadowmount, and food, as we understand it, is scarce. There's a limit to the comforts sorcery can provide."

"There's also a limit as to what we can share if you're undersupplied," Rochelle said. "You can't count on us to make up the difference."

Zaria and Nessa exchanged a look.

"Anything that helps us get there I'm in favor of," Zaria said.

Nessa responded with a brief nod and continued eating her lunch.

"Just show us where the supply room is," Zaria said to Lumina, speaking around Nessa.

"I'd be happy to," Lumina said.

When the meal was finished, Marlys and her company helped with the cleanup, as usual. She was pleasantly surprised that Nessa and Zaria helped clear the table and clean it. Neither group spoke to the other, however.

After all had been cleaned and put away, Lumina led Nessa and Zaria away, presumably to receive their coins. The others returned to their rooms, where they continued to pack and repack their bundles. With the number of days and kinds of hardships they would face unknown, they frequently changed their minds about what and how much each would carry.

"Some time, we will simply have to settle on the amount of supplies each of us is able to carry and leave it at that," Serena said.

"We have at least a two day journey to the foothills of the Mountains of Wrath, even with shortening distances," Marlys said. "Who knows how much time we will need to get through the sorcerous barrier, and then to the Shadowmount?"

"I'm not counting on finding any food in the region," Tir said.

"We can always come back here if we run out of supplies," Rochelle said.

"Though I plan to keep pressing forward unless our need is dire," Marlys said.

The others nodded.

"The waycakes are small and we should be able to carry at least enough for maybe ten days," Serena said. "That should be more than sufficient."

Tir faced her. "What about water?"

"We should each carry a full waterskin," Serena said. "We can't count on finding streams, or condensing water from the air, or digging until we strike an underground pool."

Rochelle looked over what she had gathered, spread out on her bed. "Waycakes, bedding, warm clothes, rope, grappling hooks. I think I have everything, then, except the waterskins."

"Yes, I think it's time to settle on what we have and just pack it," Marlys said.

"Do you still have the key from Hilltop?" Tir asked.

"Yes," Marlys said. "It's with my things."

"Let's head to the supply room and get the waterskins," Serena said.

When they entered the room, they saw Lumina, Nessa, and Zaria gathered around a table. Various supplies lay on the tabletop.

"I think this is what you need to carry," Lumina said to them. She looked up when Marlys and her companions entered. "Something else you need?"

"One more item," Serena said. "A waterskin for each of us."

Zaria turned to Nessa. "We're adding those, too."

Nessa gestured at the supplies she had gathered and turned to Marlys. "Since you seem to know what you're doing, what else do you have that's not here that we need?"

While Lumina went to a cabinet to hand out waterskins, Marlys looked over the supplies on the table. She looked up at Nessa. "Did you bring waycakes from Wishborne?"

"They're with our other things in our rooms," Zaria said.

Nessa sighed. "We were going to leave without them, but somehow Brianna slipped a couple of packages into our carry bags."

"Lucky for you she did," Tir said.

Nessa threw him an exasperated look but said nothing.

"How long were you planning to stay?" Marlys said. "Once we've filled our waterskins, all we have to do is finish packing. We can leave as early as tomorrow but are willing to stay here until you're ready."

"We don't want to wait, either," Nessa said. "If we're going, we may as well go."

"Let's plan to talk after dinner tonight," Marlys suggested.

"What is there to talk about?" Nessa sounded wary.

"If we're to work as a team," Marlys said, "we need a team strategy. That means each of us needs to be clear as to how to work together, leaving no one out."

Nessa seemed to relax. She nodded.

After dinner, they all helped clean up, but left their teacups, saucers, and the teapot on the table for their return. Lumina thanked them for their help and told them she would finish in the kitchen while they held their discussion in the dining room. She put on a kettle of water to boil and gave them a plate of cakes to take to the next room with them.

They settled, as usual, with Nessa and Zaria on one side of the table, Marlys and her companions on the other side.

Marlys set folded hands on the table. "First, we are resolved to keep on, barring catastrophe. Are you equally determined?"

Nessa glanced at Zaria before answering. "Yes, we are."

"Good," Marlys said. "Did you have a route in mind or shall we lead the way?"

"I had thought that our host, here, would give us directions," Nessa said.

"You didn't look at the maps and drawings at Castlemount?" Serena asked.

"Maps?" Zaria said. "What maps?"

"The maps in the cabinet of drawers in the library," Serena said.

"The artwork on the wall and in the library were revealing as well," Tir said.

"We spent our time there reading the spell books," Nessa said, "and opened one drawer with various sketches to get the snowflake key. We didn't notice any maps, and the artwork just seemed to be for decoration."

"It seemed to have a bit more significance than that," Rochelle said.

"No one told us," Zaria said.

"My impression is that part of the exercise of the Spell Passage is to make discoveries on one's own," Tir said.

"I thought the point was for the stations along the passage to give us the information we needed to find the Library of Sorcery," Nessa said.

Serena nodded. "The hosts answer questions, and make their resources available, but we have to be the ones to do the exploring."

"This may surprise you," Marlys said to Nessa and Zaria, "but the hosts don't know where the Library of Sorcery is, either. They can give general directions and general advice, but don't have any more idea of where it is exactly than we do."

"Yes, that does surprise me," Nessa grumbled.

"We also had a long conversation at Woodlands with High Sorcerer Ware and Sorcerer Junia before going on the Spell Passage," Marlys said. "They, and one of their apprentices, have also tried to find the Library of Sorcery. Although they were not successful, they did give us information about the approach to the Mountains of Wrath. Have you ever spoken to them about this?"

Nessa sighed. "No."

"Then you have no objection to us leading the way?" Marlys said.

"No, but I need some direction to form an end point," Nessa said. "Can you draw me a map?"

Marlys leaned back in her chair and faced the open doorway to the kitchen. "Lumina?"

She came to the door promptly. "Yes?"

"Do you have a map showing the area between here and the Mountains of Wrath?" Marlys said. "Since Durand said he traveled through there, I thought he might have left a map or notes."

Lumina nodded. "Yes, I have a very old map that Durand consulted before his journey. I can show it to you if you wish."

"We do," Marlys said.

"Now, or later?" Lumina asked.

"At your convenience," Marlys said.

"Now." Nessa noticed Marlys's raised eyebrow and added in a strained voice, "If you please. If it's convenient."

Lumina smiled. "I'd be happy to show you now."

Lumina escorted them to the supply room. She pulled out a drawer set in a storage chest. "The map is very ancient. You can look, but please do not touch it."

The others gathered around. Rochelle reached for a lantern and held it over the open drawer to give them more light.

Their host passed a hand over the paper. "As you can see, to reach the Mountains of Wrath, you will need to travel a distance north from here, and then take a path to the west-northwest."

Tir pointed, bringing his finger close to, but not touching, the map. "These cliffs mark the foothills, and beyond that, the Shadowmount."

Lumina nodded. "Those who have traveled that far say you can see the Shadowmount in the far distance. Some have claimed to see a structure at the Shadowmount which may be the Library of Sorcery."

Nessa scrutinized the map. "Is everything according to scale? No exaggeration of distances?"

Lumina turned to her. "Yes. It's a true representation of distance."

Nessa nodded solemnly. "Then I can follow the route. Do you have a blank paper about the size of the map? And can you provide pen and ink?"

"I can." Lumina went elsewhere in the room and quickly brought back the materials.

Nessa took them and set them on the top of the cabinet. She began to sketch, looking alternately from the map to the paper.

Marlys and her companions looked on, fascinated.

"Making a fair copy," Tir said. "That's quite a talent."

Nessa spoke without pausing in her work. "Enhanced by a simple household spell."

"I admire your ingenuity," Serena said.

Nessa raised an eyebrow briefly but gave no other acknowledgement.

"I don't see any markings indicating forests or trees," Zaria said.

"There are few in that region," Lumina said. "It's largely bare, rocky ground with occasional patches of grass. Animals are seldom seen."

When Nessa finished, she dried the ink—a simple household spell—and rolled up the paper. She nodded at Lumina. "Thank you."

"I'm here to assist," Lumina said modestly, and closed the drawer. She took the ink and pen and returned them to their places.

Nessa turned to Marlys. "Will your group be ready to go tomorrow?"

Lumina, apparently overhearing, said, "The waterskins are filled. I'll bring them."

Marlys nodded at Lumina and turned to Nessa. "Yes, we can go after breakfast."

Nessa touched Zaria's arm. "Let's finish packing, then."

Part III:
The Library of Sorcery

Chapter 20

After breakfast the next morning, Lumina helped them prepare to leave. Marlys and her companions did not need much assistance. Lumina spent most of the time helping Nessa and Zaria, showing how to best distribute the weight of their carry packs and waterskins. When Nessa and Zaria saw the others holding walking staffs, they each grabbed one for themselves.

Lumina stood at the door and waved a farewell as the visiting sorcerers walked away from the fortress. She went back inside and shut the door behind her only when they turned a corner on the path.

"Not out of range of the orbs yet," Tir remarked after failing to kindle a sorcerous light.

"I wish they'd get rid of those orbs," Nessa grumbled. "Maybe they had a use at one time, but we're all pledged never to harm another sorcerer now."

"I don't know," Rochelle said. "I found it a refreshing change not to have to rely on sorcery."

"I didn't become a sorcerer to go back to using only household spells," Nessa said. "I felt restrained."

"It does save effort," Tir said. "Casting major spells can be exhausting."

"As for me, I missed the ability to read speedily," Serena said.

Tir continued to attempt to kindle a sorcerous light about every ten paces. Once he succeeded, they all stopped.

Nessa stepped forward, raised an arm, and described a circle. A ring of spinning light appeared ahead of them. Keeping her arm extended, Nessa turned to the others. "Zaria will go first. Follow her. And don't ask me to teach this to you."

Marlys and her companions looked from one to the other with puzzled expressions.

"Didn't occur to me," Rochelle said.

"Unless you offer to show us, we aren't going to ask," Serena reassured her.

"Good." Nessa turned back to the sorcerous end point.

Zaria stepped through the ring. Marlys followed. She found herself standing on a rocky flat with scrub brush here and there. Taking a few steps forward, she turned to see Rochelle, Serena, and Tir step through.

Finally, Nessa appeared. She turned, gestured, and the ring dissolved. Leaning back, she loosened the straps on her carry bag and waterskin before lowering them slowly to the ground. "This is as far as I can go for now," she said while rummaging in her pack. Taking out a foldable seat, she opened it and sat on it.

Zaria did the same.

Tir looked up and around. "The sun's position has changed drastically. Either we traveled a long distance or we traveled a long time."

"Both," Nessa said.

"I'm even more impressed with your spell now," Marlys said. "I had no sensation of the passage of time or distance."

Nessa threw Marlys an exasperated look.

"May as well make ourselves comfortable," Tir said.

The rest of the party put down their packs and took out their foldable seats.

Rochelle looked around. She pointed to the west-northwest. "Those cliffs in the distance must be the leading edge of the Mountains of Wrath."

Tir pointed north. "More mountains there."

"I can see the top of the Pinnacle fortress in the distant south," Serena said.

"Forest to the east," Marlys said. "Dense forest, tall trees."

"Nothing here but rocks and some small bushy plants," Zaria said glumly. "I'd call it a desert, but there's no sand."

"A little gravel, but no sand, yes," Tir said.

"There has to be some soil and moisture to support the scrub brush," Serena said, "but other than that, it's hard ground for quite a distance."

"Anyone for lunch?" Rochelle said. "I'm hungry."

Tir rummaged through this pack. "What shall it be, waycake or the fresh food we brought from Pinnacle?"

"Doesn't matter to me," Rochelle said. "Household spells will keep the food fresh, so we don't have to eat what we brought from Pinnacle right away."

Everyone opened their packs, took out enough food for a meal, and started to eat.

Tir poured water into a small ceramic teapot and heated it. "Anyone for tea?"

Marlys and Serena held out their cups.

"I'll stick with plain water, but thanks," Rochelle said.

When they finished, they cleaned up using household spells. Zaria stood and looked around, turning in a circle. She inclined her head toward Nessa. "It's plain that we're not going to reach a dwelling or any kind of structure today, or maybe even tomorrow."

"Is that a problem? We...," Tir gestured to the others in his group, "...planned on being outdoors for several days."

"So, what?" Zaria said. "You just go potty on the ground?"

Marlys and Serena exchanged puzzled looks.

"You don't know how to spell a commode?" Serena said. "Granted, you can make a nicer one with sorcery, but you can set up a perfectly functional one with a household spell."

"I've never had to," Zaria said.

"No one ever taught me," Nessa said.

"No one taught me, either," Tir said, "I figured out how to do it when I was six years old."

Nessa threw him a withering look.

Rochelle put her hands on her knees and levered herself to a standing position. She motioned to Zaria. "Here, I'll show you." She walked away from their camp to a place where the scrub brush was tall enough and thick enough to obscure the view of someone sitting. Zaria and Nessa followed.

While Rochelle explained the procedure, Tir leaned over to Marlys and Serena and said in a low voice, "Are we going to have to teach them basic spells now?"

"We all have gaps in our knowledge," Marlys said. "Nessa brought us here farther and faster than we could with the distance-shortening spell. We need to make allowances for each other."

Tir sighed. "Very well. I only hope that this doesn't become a habit."

When Rochelle, Zaria, and Nessa returned, Marlys turned to them. "We usually rest a while after the midday meal."

Without looking at Marlys, Nessa said in a faint voice, "We do, too."

Rochelle took out her bedroll and stretched out on it. Tir also took out his bedroll, but left it bound and placed it between him and a nearby rock. He leaned back and practiced lighting spells. Serena stood and walked around. Marlys took out a journal from her pack and began to write.

"Keeping a record of your journey?" Zaria asked.

"Yes. As High Sorcerer, I kept a daily journal of the activities in Goldenvalley. That book remained at the fortress, of course, but I thought I would bring something with me to record my thoughts."

Zaria did not answer. She reached into her pack, brought out a piece of cloth, and began to stitch.

Tir looked over at her. "Needlepoint? I remember you stitching pillowcases at Goldenvalley."

Zaria ignored him.

Tir looked over at Marlys, inclined his head briefly in Zaria's direction, and went back to practicing spells.

Nessa took out a thin piece of charcoal, paper, and a thin board to rest the paper against. She began to sketch. As she worked, she sang softly to herself.

"You have a nice voice," Tir remarked.

Nessa stopped singing, looked briefly at Tir with a bland expression, and returned to her sketching and singing.

Eventually, Marlys put her journal away and stood, stretching. "I'm ready to resume. What you do think, Nessa?"

Nessa put her materials back in her pack. "Yes, I think it's time to go on."

When the others had hoisted their packs and gathered together, Nessa extended her arm to the west-northwest. "Now that I can see our destination, casting the spell will be easier."

Once again, they all walked through the glowing ring that Nessa had formed. When they emerged, the foothills, though still at a distance, were visibly closer. The sun had almost reached the tops of the Mountains of Wrath.

Tir looked in that direction and cast a spell. "Even with the far-seeing spell, I can't quite locate the Shadowmount yet." He waved a hand. "Though I presume it's somewhere in that direction."

"We'll see it soon enough, no doubt," Rochelle said.

Nessa put down her pack and waterskin. "This is as far as we go today."

"This is good progress, thank you," Marlys said.

Nessa glanced at her but did not answer.

When they were settled, they again took food out of their packs for a meal. Marlys, Rochelle, and Serena gathered enough of the nearby brush to make a campfire, which Tir lit and monitored. Zaria took a skewer out of her pack and took advantage of the flame to warm her chicken leg and bread.

"We'd be happy to use sorcery to heat your food for you," Tir said.

"I like the taste of food roasted over a fire," Zaria said.

"So do I," Rochelle said, who bought out her own skewers.

During the meal, Serena said, "I'd advise everyone to take a long, leisurely walk between now and retiring. We've not used our muscles to any great extent today, and we need to keep them strong and limber for the journey ahead. We can't count on always being able to shorten distances."

"Or being able to use sorcery at all," Nessa grumbled.

"Good point," Tir said.

After they ate, Tir maintained the fire, keeping it burning and within bounds.

Rochelle stood and brushed herself off. "I have an idea. Instead of taking a hike, how about a circle dance? That should keep us fit."

Marlys turned to Nessa and Zaria, expecting them to protest, but they looked at each other, shrugged, and nodded.

Almost everyone in the various regions learned some sort of circle dance in childhood. At just about every regional center Marlys knew of, it was a common form of evening entertainment.

They took hands around the fire and Rochelle led the way. Marlys noticed that even Zaria and Nessa smiled and laughed as they made their way around the campfire.

The sun had set and the stars had come out by the time they ran out of energy. They sat around the fire, resting.

Zaria reached into her pack and brought out a cloak. "It got chilly fast."

"That often happens in rocky terrain," Marlys said.

Serena stood. "I think I'll do some more walking and exploring."

"Don't go too long," Tir said. "I'll be setting up the wards soon. I doubt that we'll be bothered by animals or anything else, but it's a reasonable precaution."

Serena bent down until her head was near Tir's. "I'll just use a pass-through spell if they're set up."

Tir grinned as Serena walked away.

Rochelle looked up. "Bright stars. No moon tonight."

"There'll be a sliver of a moon later, I think," Marlys said.

Nessa unrolled her bedding and held it up. "Is there a trick to this?"

"I'll show you," Marlys said.

At the same time Marlys showed Nessa how and where to set up her bedroll for maximum comfort, Rochelle did the same for Zaria.

"Are you going to be warm enough without sorcery?" Rochelle asked her.

"I have plenty of warm wraps," Zaria said. "But I'll call if I need to."

Rochelle nodded and returned to her own pack.

Serena came back not long after, and the rest of them settled around the campfire to sleep.

The wards sounded no alarm during the night. After eating breakfast, re-packing, and extinguishing the fire, Nessa created another end point and they set out again. With each jump, the Mountains of Wrath loomed closer. By midday on the third day, they stepped out within paces of the cliffs.

After removing her packs, Nessa said, "I think we have reached the edge of the Mountains of Wrath."

Tir cast the far-seeing spell. "I can see the Shadowmount now. As they told us at Woodlands, I think I can make out what could be a building on the side, but it's indistinct, as if lost in the mists."

The others also turned in that direction.

"Could be anything," Rochelle said. "Maybe it's a structure, maybe it's ruins, maybe it's just rocks arranged in such a way that they resemble a building."

Marlys nodded. "We probably won't know until we get closer."

Rochelle walked to the cliffs and looked up. "At home, we have climbers who can go up a rock face using the narrowest of cracks for a handhold or foothold. I'm not seeing anything here that I can make use of."

"There's the climbing spell we learned at Overlook," Serena said.

Nessa turned to her. "What climbing spell?"

Serena faced Nessa. "You didn't learn the climbing spell at the tower?"

"No. We saw it in the spell book, but I couldn't see that it would help us find the Library."

"We tried it outside the area of sorcery cancellation just to learn a new spell," Marlys said. "Kayli and Durand taught us."

Nessa threw up her hands. "Well, they didn't teach us."

"It's not hard to learn." Rochelle nodded toward Zaria. "Once we're up, we can use the rope and pull Zaria up."

"Wonderful," Zaria said glumly.

Rochelle walked toward the cliffs, stretching out her arm to touch the rock. Abruptly, she stopped. "Uh, oh."

"That doesn't sound good," Tir said.

Rochelle turned around. "There's a very strong sorcerous barrier here. I can feel it."

"Just as Ware and Junia told us," Marlys said.

"Well, we can't touch the cliffs," Rochelle said.

"Maybe we can use the climbing spell to climb up next to the side?" Tir suggested.

Nessa let out a heavy sigh. "I can see the top. I'll just create an end point."

The others turned to her.

"Worth a try," Serena said.

"'A try'?" Nessa's brow furrowed. "How can it not work?"

"Maybe the same way the heating spell didn't work at Stronghold?" Tir said.

Nessa sighed again. "Let's sit and eat lunch. We have the entire rest of the day to try it."

After a meal and a rest, Nessa stepped back from the cliffs until she could see the top. "All right. I should be able to create an end point that will get us on secure footing." She cast the spell, rotating her arm. Suddenly, she fell backward as if pushed, landing on her seat.

Marlys hurried over and knelt beside her, putting a hand on her back for support. "Are you injured?"

"What in the universe was that?" She rubbed her arm. "My arm is still tingling."

"That isn't the only way up," Tir said. "Let me try the climbing spell."

He walked as close to the cliffs as he could, looked up, cast the spell, and lifted his leg. His foot hovered in the air, lowered, and met ground again. He turned and shrugged.

"Can you cast a spell at all?" Zaria asked.

Serena kindled a sorcerous light. "Yes."

Rochelle took out her rope. "Let me see if I can use sorcery to get the rope to the top and anchor it." She cast the spell and threw the rope upwards. Immediately, it came down again. She gathered the rope and shrugged.

"Plainly, we can use sorcery," Nessa said. "We just can't use the spells we know of to reach the top of the cliffs."

"Well, we were warned it wouldn't be easy," Marlys said.

"I'm not giving up," Nessa said.

"Neither are we," Serena said. "If the spells we know won't allow us to breach the barrier, we'll just have to invent a new one."

Chapter 21

"Invent a new spell?" Nessa said. "That could take months."

"Not necessarily," Serena said.

Marlys sat next to Nessa and gestured. "Let's all sit and think about this." When the others had gathered around, she continued, "Going through the Spell Passage was supposed to prepare us for this. What did we learn that could help us?"

"Do you still have the key?" Serena said.

As Marlys rummaged through her pack, Nessa said, "What key?"

"The key we got at Hilltop," Marlys said, holding it up. "We found it in a hidden room. Even Hilde didn't know it was there."

"I've never seen a keyhole that size," Zaria said.

"The shape may be symbolic," Marlys said, "signifying that it unlocks or opens something. It seems to be spelled."

"How can you tell?" Zaria asked.

"Over at Hilltop, it glowed and vibrated," Serena said. "It has energy."

"It's not glowing now," Nessa said.

"No," Marlys agreed.

Serena stretched out a hand. "Can I take it over to the cliff and see whether it has any effect?"

Marlys handed it over. "By all means, give it a try."

Serena took the key, stood, and walked over to the cliff until the barrier stopped her. She held the key up.

"Nothing," Rochelle said.

Serena shook her head, walked back, sat, and handed the key to Marlys. "No vibration, no glow."

"Maybe the key is supposed to help us once we get to the Library of Sorcery," Tir said.

"If we ever get there," Zaria said.

Marlys put the key back in her bag. "We'll get there."

Zaria turned to the cliffs. "What if I throw everything I have at it...become a sorcerer."

"No," everyone else said at once.

Zaria crossed her arms in front of her. "I'm getting tired of being an apprentice, having everyone else do things for me. I want to do sorcery on my own."

Rochelle reached out and put a hand on Zaria's shoulder. Zaria wrenched away.

"We all were apprentices once," Marlys said. "We know exactly how you're feeling. It isn't a burden to us to help you. You'll become a sorcerer eventually."

Zaria blew out a breath.

Nessa turned to her. "I couldn't have done this without you, Zaria. You know that. You've been my only friend all this time. I wouldn't keep you from becoming a sorcerer. But this is not the way."

"We can't deny that Junia told us that she became a sorcerer by attempting—and failing, I may add—to get past the cliffs," Serena said. "But there was another apprentice with her and Ware who tried to awaken her sorcery here and failed. She said she would not recommend it, and, more to the point, Junia said the same."

Zaria looked down. Her shoulders relaxed a little.

"If I may make a suggestion," Tir said, "perhaps we should give up trying to get past the cliffs...."

"Never," Nessa interjected.

Tir held up a finger. "...for now, and just spend the rest of the day relaxing. A good night's rest could give us fresh ideas when tomorrow comes."

Marlys saw nods all around.

Rochelle got out her bedroll. "I'm taking a nap."

The others followed suit.

Marlys stretched out on her bedroll and closed her eyes. She had not realized she had slept until she felt a reverberation, like an earthquake through the air instead of the ground. Raising herself on an elbow, she turned toward the cliffs and saw Zaria there, arms outstretched, groaning. Immediately, she scrambled to her feet and ran in that direction.

Marlys heard Nessa shout behind her. "Zaria, no!"

Reaching Zaria just as she started to fall backwards, Marlys put an arm around her waist to prevent her from striking her head on the ground. Zaria's body shook.

Rochelle arrived. Supporting Zaria between her and Marlys, they slowly walked Zaria back to the encampment.

"Breathe, breathe," Marlys said gently. "You aren't dying, it only feels that way. You'll be fine. You just need some rest."

Nessa hovered as Rochelle and Marlys lowered Zaria onto her bedroll. "I'll take care of her from here."

Marlys and Rochelle drew back and went to sit next to Tir and Serena.

Rochelle sighed. "Reminds me of all the stupid things I did before becoming a sorcerer."

"I was remembering all the stupid things, I did, too," Tir said.

"How badly was she affected?" Serena asked.

"Shock, definitely," Marlys said. "But I didn't sense anything beyond that."

"Good," Serena said. "After all the lectures we give apprentices about not trying to force an awakening of sorcery, you'd think they'd hesitate more."

"The problem is," Marlys said, "a forced awakening sometimes works. Remember Gweneth? So we always have apprentices who think they'll be the exception."

Rochelle nodded and sighed. "Well, maybe Zaria will think twice if she's tempted again. She's still an apprentice and all she did was exhaust herself."

They turned to watch as Nessa tucked a blanket around Zaria, who seemed to be sleeping peacefully. Nessa returned to her own bedroll, sitting with her knees up, arms around her raised legs. She buried her face in her pant legs and began to weep.

Marlys walked to Nessa's bedroll, took the blanket there, and arranged it around Nessa's shoulders. Sitting next to Nessa, Marlys put an arm around her. She did not protest, but continued to weep. Marlys remained silent.

When Nessa's weeping eased, Marlys stood and returned to her companions.

"You said nothing to her?" Rochelle asked as Marlys sat.

"No," Marlys said. "Anything I said would have simply annoyed her." She glanced over to Nessa, who grasped her waterskin and took a drink. "She almost lost her friend, her only friend. I know how it feels to feel friendless among sorcerers. She must feel exhausted from her fruitless efforts."

Rochelle took a breath. "I hope you won't think me cruel if I say I don't feel sorry for her. Her problems are of her own making."

"No, I don't think you're cruel, Rochelle," Marlys said. "You're right, of course. But we can't force her to realize the futility of her actions. She has to come to that conclusion herself."

Tir nodded in Nessa's direction. "Her waterskin is nearly empty. As is mine."

"As are all of ours," Rochelle said.

"I've walked around every place we have rested," Serena said, "using the dowsing spell. But I haven't found a spring, underground stream, or even a significant water table."

"I've looked, as well," Tir said. "I can't extract water from the air, either. Too dry."

"There aren't any succulents around," Serena said. "If we found those, we could get enough water by eating them, but there's nothing around here but dry brush."

Marlys nodded. "Desert plants can thrive with the rare rainfalls..."

"Desert bloom," Serena affirmed.

"...but I don't think we can count on a rainstorm," Marlys finished.

Rochelle pulled back the flap of her carry pack and looked inside. "I have maybe five days' worth of waycakes, ten if we're careful." She turned back to her companions. "But we need water."

"I can see why sorcerers give up here," Serena said. "It's not only the sorcerous barrier, it's the lack of food and water."

Tir crossed his arms in front of him. "Can't conjure those," he said glumly.

Serena turned to Marlys. "What now? Do we go back?"

Marlys sighed. "We won't die of thirst if we stay here another day. Maybe something will occur to us."

"There are the mountains to the north," said a low voice.

They turned to Nessa, still resting her head on her upraised knees.

"That won't help us if the barrier rings the Mountains of Wrath," Tir said.

"No," Nessa agreed, raising her head and facing them, "but we might find food and water there, enough to resupply and come back. I've scanned them with the far-seeing spell, and there is abundant plant life there. It should be within reach of my farthest end point, though it may take more than one jump."

Marlys nodded. "That could work."

"Thanks for crediting me with some brains," Nessa said sarcastically. She stood, stretched, and walked around their campsite.

Zaria had recovered by dinnertime. They gathered around the fire and ate an adequate meal, but only drank a little water. The next morning, at breakfast, the little water they had ran out.

"I wish I could have saved some, but I had to have a least a little," Tir remarked.

"It's the same with all of us," Marlys said.

They packed up in preparation for going north. As they did, Nessa hummed a tune.

Marlys looked at Serena. "That sounds familiar."

Without looking toward them, Nessa answered, "Yes, it's a tune I learned at Heathervale. Petra and I sang along with the crystals there. And no, I'm not stopping if you don't like it."

"We aren't asking you to," Rochelle said. "It's a lovely tune."

Nessa raised an eyebrow and went from humming to singing the notes. "Aaah, aaah, aaah...."

Tir pointed. "Marlys, your pack is moving."

"Could an animal have crawled in there during the night?" Rochelle said.

Marlys lifted her pack. Without opening it, she said, "No, it's not an animal." She reached in and drew out the key. "It's this. It's glowing."

Serena turned to the cliffs. "There's a change in the barrier. I feel it."

Nessa stopped singing and joined the others as they strode to the cliffs.

Serena reached out a hand. "Yes...."

A force pushed them all back.

"...and no," Serena said.

"The key isn't glowing now," Tir said.

Marlys motioned to Nessa. "Start singing again." When Nessa faced her, Marlys added, "Please?"

Nessa straightened up, threw her shoulders back, and began to sing the notes as if she were in an opera.

"The key's glowing again," Tir said.

Serena rushed to the cliffs and put a hand on the cliff face. "Yes!" She looked up. "We can climb now."

Nessa stopped singing, taking a breath.

Serena stepped back from the cliff face. "I have a feeling the barrier will stay down only for a brief time if Nessa stops singing." She rejoined the others.

Marlys held up the key. The glow slowly faded.

Serena faced the cliffs. "Yes. The barrier's back. I can feel it."

Nessa threw up her hands.

"How long can you sing without a rest?" Marlys asked.

"Oh, I can sing five, maybe ten verses of a song at a time," Nessa said. "But that's a very high cliff. Can I sing long enough for us to get up there?"

"Can you make your end point?" Serena asked.

"I can try." Nessa had to back up at least fifty paces before she could see the top of the cliff. She started to sing, cast the spell, extended her arm, and immediately drew it back. "Apparently not," she said, rubbing her arm.

"Need help in healing?" Marlys asked.

Nessa shook her arm. "No, it's fine."

"It seems then, that your singing is the only way up," Marlys said.

Nessa shrugged.

"How do we organize this?" Rochelle said. "My first thought was that the four of us sorcerers get to the top and let down a rope for Zaria, but it's too high. I could climb up with the step spell carrying Zaria on my back."

Zaria sighed and rubbed her forehead.

"Would you rather stay here?" Tir asked her.

Zaria waved a hand in resignation.

"We need to teach Nessa the step spell," Serena said. "The question is, can she sing and spell at the same time?"

"I can do two things at once," Nessa said dryly.

"But is the singing a spell?" Serena said. "We can cast a spell and let it take hold, and then cast a second spell, but the singing is continuous, and so is the step spell. Unless you have talents we don't, sorcerers can't sustain two spells at once."

Tir turned to Serena. "She can try to do both at once before we attempt the ascent."

Nessa gestured at them. "Show me the step spell and I'll try it."

Serena taught Nessa the spell. Nessa cast the spell, started to sing, and then began to ascend. After she had reached a height above the others, she descended and stopped singing. She spread her hands and faced the others.

"Good," Serena said.

"Here's what I propose," Rochelle said. "We distribute my and Zaria's packs among Tir, Serena, and Marlys. They're lighter now, and we've been using a spell to help carry the weight anyway. I'll take Zaria. We ascend side-by-side: me between Tir and Marlys, Nessa between Serena and Marlys. Then if any of us need help, we can lean on the others."

As they made the preparations, Tir leaned in Marlys's direction. "What happens when we reach the top?"

"Let's talk about that when we get there," Marlys said.

When they were ready, Nessa turned to the others. "You're free to sing, too."

"None of us carry a tune as well as you," Tir said, "and we didn't memorize the tune as you did."

"I don't know how you can avoid it," Nessa said. "It's been on my mind ever since I first heard it."

"Is it unpleasant?" Marlys asked.

"No," Nessa said. "In fact, I find it soothing. It only comes to mind now and again, but I've never forgotten it."

"Perhaps one needs a certain amount of musical ability for the tune to take hold," Rochelle said.

"Or," Nessa said, "the willingness to do the work of memorization."

Marlys nodded. "That could be the case. Shall we start?"

Nessa began to sing. Marlys had put a string through the key and wore it as if it were a necklace. Side-by-side, they approached the cliff. The climbers each cast the step spell and began to ascend.

Chapter 22

Progress was deliberately slow, as no one wanted to get too far ahead of the others. But they reached the top at last. They found themselves standing on a narrow ridge, a few paces wide at most, overlooking a steep slope downward.

Nessa, still singing, turned to Marlys as Zaria slipped off Rochelle's back and found her footing.

"Let's take a few steps from the ridge to be safe," Marlys said.

Nessa nodded as they all carefully descended down the grassy incline.

When Nessa stopped singing, they all turned to the ridge.

"I can feel the barrier returning," Serena said.

"Yes," Tir said. "Fortunately, it doesn't seem to extend to us."

With their backs to the east, they turned their gaze westward. Marlys saw a U-shaped terrain. The land dipped sharply from where they stood, to a wide valley. There she could see, slightly southward, a village. All around stood orchards and croplands. Flocks grazed on grasses. Rivers and streams, flowing southward, watered the plains. To the north, the land sloped upwards to the northern mountains. Westward, the land rose again to the Mountains of Wrath, with the Shadowmount prominent among them.

"Are you using the far-seeing spell?" Tir asked, pointing. "I see the ledge at the side of the Shadowmount, and there's definitely a structure there."

"The Library of Sorcery?" Nessa said.

"We think so," Serena said.

"It's going to take more than a day to get there," Marlys said.

"Then let's start," Nessa said.

"Let's redistribute the packs first," Rochelle said.

Once they were again outfitted, Nessa spelled an end point. "We're going to step out at the edge of the village, there."

When they emerged, Marlys looked around and saw that Nessa had placed them on a cobblestone road just outside the cluster of buildings that formed the village. Fortunately, no one was on the road at the moment.

"Where now?" Tir asked.

"Let's find an inn, at least," Zaria said. "I'm tired of sleeping on the ground."

"Let's just follow the road for now," Marlys said. "It's a small village, so we should be able to find an inn just by walking around."

They had not gone far when they began to pass villagers, who stared at them curiously, but did not approach or call out to them.

Tir pointed ahead. "That seems to be the village square, with a public well at the center."

"Good. I could use a drink of water," Nessa said.

They approached the well, a circular pool with stone sides. A fountain welled up in the middle. A number of villagers had gathered around, using a designated bucket to fill pitchers, vases, and other containers. When there was an opening, all five of them gathered around the stone ridge and filled their waterskins.

A woman, holding her filled container, approached Marlys. "I haven't seen you before."

"We're from a distant land," Marlys said. "Five of us are sorcerers and the sixth is an apprentice. We've come to visit the Library of Sorcery."

"You aren't Librarians, then?" the woman said.

"No," Marlys said cordially.

"The Librarians aren't scheduled to come for some days yet," another woman remarked.

"We were planning on traveling there," Marlys said.

"It's a long way," the first woman said, "though I understand sorcerers can travel quickly."

"We can," Serena said.

"Can you point us to an inn?" Zaria remarked.

Several of the onlookers pointed to a large two story building.

"Thank you," Marlys said.

All six of them took long draughts from their waterskins before heading toward the inn. The door was open. They stepped inside. The main room was airy, high-ceilinged, well lit. The floors and tables were clean, mostly unoccupied, and the windows were large and dustless.

A man standing behind a counter called to them. "What can I help you with, visitors?"

Marlys approached the counter, and heard the others following her. "We're looking for rooms, and meals."

He smiled warmly. "Of course. I require a small payment in advance."

Marlys saw Nessa open her mouth and put a hand on her shoulder before she could blurt out that services should be free to sorcerers. Nessa met Marlys's eyes and sighed.

Meanwhile, Serena fished into a pocket and brought out coins. She extended her hand. "Would you take these?"

The man, and the woman standing next to him, scrutinized the coins and shook their heads.

"They're pure gold," Serena affirmed cordially.

The man shook his head again. "Sorry. I don't recognize these. You might consult the goldsmith. He might give you something for those."

Serena nodded and put the coins back into her pocket.

"Is there any way we can earn money?" Marlys asked.

"Oh, yes." The woman pointed outside. Marlys saw her left hand was bandaged. "There's a board in the city square. People who will pay for help post notices there."

"We posted a notice that we need someone to milk the cows and goats, at least for today" the man said. "My wife hurt her hand cutting a chicken up for dinner, and can't milk very well. I can't do it at all."

Marlys reached out over the counter. "Can I see your hand? I should be able to heal it."

The woman exchanged a look with the man and turned back to Marlys with a skeptical expression.

Marlys nodded. "I understand. You're used to the Librarians healing you, and we're not sorcerers you're familiar with."

"If you don't mind my saying so," the woman said,"you don't look like a sorcerer."

The man turned to the woman. "Maybe she means she can do household spells?"

"What do you expect a sorcerer to look like?" Marlys asked.

"They have a certain...presence," said the man. "It's hard to describe. You know it when you see it."

"We're not from here, which means we may seem different, but we are true sorcerers." Marlys kindled a sorcerous light, which spread throughout the room.

The woman shrugged.

"My name is Marlys, by the way," she said, and quickly introduced the others.

"I'm Anya...and this is my husband, Gerald."

Marlys smiled. "Pleased to meet you. May I see your hand now?"

Anya extended her arm. Marlys took it gently, removed the bandages, examined the wound, closed her eyes briefly, and cast a healing spell. The wound gradually closed, the skin knitted together. Marlys let go of Anya's hand.

Anya rubbed her left hand with her right. "It feels good."

"It should be healed now," Marlys said.

"Thank you," Anya said.

"We're always glad to be of service," Marlys said.

Tir leaned over the counter. "By the way, I can milk both cows and goats. I'd be happy to help."

"We need the help," Anya said, "the work has piled up because I haven't been able to use my hand."

"Just show me," Tir said.

Marlys turned to Gerald as Tir and Anya disappeared through a door in the back. "Is that enough deposit to give us rooms? We can search the postings you told us about to earn enough to pay the rest."

Gerald nodded. He reached behind the counter and produced three keys. "If you don't mind doubling up, your rooms are at the top of the stairs and to the right."

"Thank you." Marlys distributed the keys.

Once they had placed their carry packs and waterskins in their rooms, they walked outside. The job board proved easy to find: it was on the other side of the public well, and people had gathered around it.

Marlys and her companions approached.

Serena surveyed the board and grasped one of the postings almost immediately. She turned to Zaria. "Sewing needed. Shall you and I try that?"

Zaria inclined her head slightly.

Paper in hand, Serena looked around. "We need to find the sewing shop."

Fortunately, those nearby overheard her and pointed. Serena smiled and thanked them before going on her way, Zaria following.

Nessa examined the board and took a posting. "Someone needs a sign painted."

A woman standing nearby said. "That would be Hemry. He's been asking around." She pointed the way, and Nessa turned in that direction.

Marlys read the postings and turned to Rochelle. "The town's cartwright needs help. What do you think?"

"Why not?"

Again, someone nearby gave directions.

At dinner that night, they all sat at a round table near a wall eating their meals. Marlys saw no empty tables once they sat down. Gradually, however, the tables emptied until only they remained.

"It's been a long day," Tir said. "I'm glad for the rest. After milking the animals, I helped with food preparation and cooking."

"The sewing shop had no lack of work," Zaria said. "The proprietor showed a needlepoint her grandmother started and left to her, and asked Serena and I if either of us had the skills to complete it. So I did."

"I kept busy mending clothes that had been left in the shop," Serena said.

"Marlys and I were repairing carts, wagons, essentially anything wheeled," Rochelle said.

"The proprietor of the shop I went to wanted something artistic," Nessa said, "so I obliged. I think he paid me well, though I don't know the value of the coins."

Gerald came over with a cup of tea. "May I join you?" The others moved to make room. He set the cup on the table, grabbed a chair, and sat between Marlys and Serena.

"I think we've earned enough to pay for room and board," Marlys said.

Gerald nodded. "You can pay me when you leave."

"We've already discussed our next steps," Marlys said. "We'll be leaving after breakfast."

"You're welcome to stay longer if you wish," Gerald said.

"We have urgent business," Nessa said.

"The Library of Sorcery?" Gerald asked.

Nessa nodded.

"We haven't had sorcerers from outside in a very long time. Before the lifetimes of my grandparents, probably even longer than that. The sorcerers we see are all from the Library."

"We understand that sorcerers from the Library of Sorcery are different, yes," Marlys said.

"Some claim they have a glow," Gerald said, "though I haven't seen it. But folks can tell, almost just by looking at them. You look like ordinary folks, as if you just ambled in from the next village over."

"I understand you don't see them very often," Serena said. "More than one person said, as you did, that they weren't expecting Librarians for days."

Gerald nodded. "That's true. They come here regularly, by calendar. They settle disputes, judge cases, heal folks if they need healing, do things such as clearing stopped up wells or make sure irrigation canals are running the right way. After a few days, they leave."

"Do you give them free lodging and meals?" Nessa asked.

"They have their own house in each village, empty when they're not here, of course. They see to their own food and clothes and such. Rarely ask for anything, but pay when they do."

"How do you get along?" Marlys asked.

"We get along well," Gerald said. "They're kindly folk, but a bit distant, if you know what I mean. As if half their mind is elsewhere. You're more like plain folk."

"I take that as a compliment," Tir said.

"I meant it as one," Gerald affirmed. "But we don't have any complaints against them. We learn in school that in ancient days, sorcerers fought with each other, did a lot of damage, but that they learned to settle down and make things better."

"We try," Marlys said.

"Are we going to see more sorcerers coming in from where you call home?" Gerald asked.

Nessa put a hand to her forehead and mumbled, "Universe forbid."

"I doubt it," Marlys answered. "Ours was a long and hazardous journey. This place wasn't easy for us to find."

"Not my business, I suppose, but thought I'd ask."

"Questions are always welcome," Marlys said.

Gerald took his cup and stood. "I wish you a restful night and pleasant dreams."

"Thank you," Marlys said. "Our best to you and Anya."

When Gerald was out of earshot, Nessa put her hand on the table. "Look, I know I'm in no position to make demands, but when we get back, if we ever get back, I'm *not* telling anyone how we got here."

"I'm not, either," Zaria added quickly.

"Anyone is welcome to travel the Spell Passage," Serena said. "But yes, I am strongly resolved not to reveal how we managed to breach the Mountains of Wrath. They can find out by themselves...or not, as the case may be."

"I don't plan to tell, either," Tir said.

"I'm not doing anyone else's work for them," Rochelle agreed.

"It's hard for a reason," Marlys said. "I'm not making it any easier."

Nessa let out a long breath. "Thank you for that."

Chapter 23

The next morning, after breakfast, they shouldered their packs and gathered at the counter. Having little idea of what the coins they had earned were worth, they simply laid what they had on the counter and allowed Gerald to take what he needed in payment. There were numerous coins left over. They pocketed their money, left the inn, and traveled down the road until they had left the last building behind. Nessa created an end point and they were on their way again.

Their experiences at other villages along the way were similar, except that they did not need to earn anything additional to pay for what they needed.

At midday on the third day, they found themselves at the foot of the Shadowmount. They stood on an empty well-kept cobblestone roadway looking up.

"There it is, the Library," Tir said. "Just beyond a retaining wall."

"Just as we saw it in the pictures at Castlemount," Rochelle said. "One level, marble exterior, stained glass windows, inset columns...."

"Beautiful," Serena said.

"The road goes up," Zaria said, "but I hope we're not climbing."

"I'll create an end point," Nessa said.

When they reached the end point, they found themselves standing at a wrought iron gate set in a tall stone wall. Through the elegantly-crafted bars, they could see a courtyard. A stone path led from the gate to the Library's front double door, which was shut. Flowers and flowering shrubs grew on either side of the path.

For a time, all of them stood there in silence, admiring it.

"Breathtaking," Rochelle said. "As if it were designed and built by the Bright Beings themselves."

"For all we know, they may have," Marlys said.

Tir pointed. "Look, there's a carillon. Chimes instead of bells, I think."

"Everything is neat, clean, and trimmed," Rochelle said. "Someone lives here."

"I don't see anyone," Tir said.

Serena put a hand on the gate and pulled. It did not move. "The gate is locked...sorcerously." She looked up. "We're not going to be able to use sorcery to get over the walls, either."

"No pull cord," Marlys said.

"How about your key?" Tir suggested.

Marlys removed the key and held it up. The gate had no lock to put it in, and it did not glow. She put it back in her pack. "No help there."

Tir stepped up to the gate. "Anyone home?" he called.

No answer.

"I'll try the song again." Nessa sang, but nothing happened.

"Let's sit and eat," Marlys said. "Perhaps someone will come along the road or come out of the Library."

They had a picnic there at the entrance, all occasionally glancing through the gate to see if anyone would appear.

When they had eaten and gathered their things again, Serena turned toward the Library, then to Marlys. "What about that calling spell Clea taught us at Landsmere?"

Marlys smiled at Serena. "Yes, that might work. Do you want to try it or shall I?"

"The calling spell I read in the books at Landsmere?" Nessa said. "That seemed trivial."

Tir grinned. "Watch and learn."

Nessa sighed and rolled her eyes.

Serena cast the spell.

They heard a sound like a pleasant warbling echoing through the mountain's rills and crevices. The carillon chimes answered in harmony.

The sound gradually faded into silence.

"Do you think they heard us?" Rochelle asked.

"Maybe they're away until evening?" Tir said.

"Wait," Marlys said calmly.

They stared at the Library's double doors. Soon, one of the doors slowly opened. A woman dressed in elegant sorcerer's robes stepped out and walked to the gate. She looked middle-aged, with short silvery hair and a round face. Marlys could see an aura surrounding her.

"Are you sorcerers? I heard a call and felt an urge to come which had to be a spell."

"Yes, we're sorcerers." Marlys introduced the others and pointed out that Zaria was an apprentice.

The woman looked them over. "I'm Genevieve. We weren't expecting anyone."

"We're from the regions south of here," Marlys said. "We came through the Spell Passage."

Genevieve's eyebrows went up. "No one has done that for several lifetimes."

"We're a determined bunch," Tir said.

Genevieve made a motion. The gate opened. "Come in, come in." As she led the way to the entrance, she said, "The other Librarians are out among the villages. Only Blair and I are here at the moment."

"Is there a head librarian?" Nessa asked.

Genevieve smiled. "That would be me." When they reached the door, she turned and gestured, closing the gate. She walked through the door and stepped to one side. Once the others had walked through, she closed the door behind them.

The entryway had a high ceiling. Abundant light streamed through stained glass windows. The veined marble walls shone. Around them, the air smelled fresh and invigorating.

Tir leaned toward Marlys and said in a low voice, "Reminds me of home."

Marlys nodded.

Genevieve extended an arm. "I'll show you to your rooms where you can settle in and rest. We'll have to go through the main library to get there."

"We would love to see the library," Serena said.

Genevieve led the way. Ahead, Marlys saw tall, decorative shelves filled with books. They crossed a threshold without a door and emerged into a room with higher, arched ceilings. Windows let in abundant light. The brown tiled floor shone. The wide aisles gave the library an airy feeling.

Marlys stopped to look at her companions, who had craned their necks, surveying the scene with expressions of awe.

In front of them, Genevieve stopped and smiled. "Most who see this for the first time are impressed."

Looking ahead, Marlys saw a well-dressed man wearing tailored pants, a tailored shirt, and a tailored shortcoat. He held an open book in his hands. An aura surrounded him, too.

Spotting the newcomers, the man grinned, put the book down, and opened his arms wide. "My brother!" he said, walking toward the group.

Tir grinned and opened his arms as well, walking forward to meet the other sorcerer.

"Well met!" the man said in an amiable tone. "I never thought I would see another male sorcerer."

They embraced. Both men patted each other on the back before separating.

"This is Blair," Genevieve said, and made introductions.

Blair held up a hand and gestured. "Welcome to the Library."

"Come," Genevieve said. "Let's get you settled in. When you are ready, you can browse to your heart's content." She started forward, the others following. "I am presuming that you came here seeking knowledge."

"We did," Serena said.

Marlys noted that Nessa and Zaria did not respond.

Each of them was shown to a small but comfortable room. Marlys noted the embroidered linens and bedspreads, made of fabric of the finest quality. The area rugs were patterned. The rooms were well-lit. Towels had been laid next to a washbowl on a vanity.

After laying down their carry packs and washing up, they all gathered again in the hallway.

Genevieve held out an arm. "Let's sit and talk. I'm sure you'd like to rest after such a long journey." She led them through corridors through a large dining/audience hall to a smaller anteroom with a round table surrounded by wooden chairs. "Make yourselves comfortable. I'll return shortly."

They sat, Nessa and Zaria next to each other. The others took chairs on either side of Marlys. They left an empty chair for Genevieve.

No one said anything until Genevieve returned carrying a tray. She set it down, sat, and served tea. "I hope you all drink tea?"

"We do," Marlys said, taking an offered cup. She reached for a small cake on a platter resting on the tray.

When everyone was served, Genevieve sat back.

"May one ask a question?" Tir said.

Genevieve smiled. "Of course. We're here to answer questions."

"I hope this won't seem rude," Tir said, "but ever since I entered, I've felt a gentle pressure on my skin, as if being caressed by sunlight."

"I have, too," Zaria said.

The others nodded.

"I thought it was just the mountain air," Marlys said.

Genevieve smiled. "As for that, the air at this altitude, outside the Library grounds, is thin and cold. Spells set in place when the Library was built thicken and warm the air here, on the road approaching, and in the caves where we store our most dangerous secrets. Occasionally, if you look outside, you'll see what appear to be geysers surging from the grounds, and fog. That's the air being replenished."

"So that's what I'm feeling," Tir said.

"The pressure on the skin is something different," Genevieve said. "We all feel it here. Those of us who live here become so accustomed to it that we don't even think about it. But newcomers, apprentices, yes, they notice it."

"Do you know what it is?" Serena asked.

"It's the power of sorcery," Genevieve said. "That's the best way to explain it. For those of us who are sorcerers, it strengthens and sharpens our abilities."

"We've heard that those who come from the Library of Sorcery have an aura about them," Serena said.

Genevieve nodded. "You will, too, if you remain here any length of time."

"Is that a spell?" Nessa asked. "Something we can take with us to strengthen the sorcerers back home?"

"No," Genevieve said. "We don't know how it works. We do know it's only active here. Again, whatever causes it was formed in the depths of the time. Ancient sorcerers? Gifts from the Bright Beings? No one has ever been able to tell."

"I, for one, am not going to question it," Rochelle said. "I'm more than happy to simply enjoy the benefits."

"We do enjoy it," Genevieve said.

"Is there an index for the spell books?" Serena asked.

Genevieve raised an eyebrow. "Are you searching for a particular spell?"

"Yes, we all are," Nessa interjected quickly.

Genevieve folded her hands on the table in front of her. "To answer your question, no, no one knows all the spells here. You saw the size of the Library. We spend our lifetimes browsing the books, learning all we can, and teaching each other what we've learned. We uncover spells all the time. But you are welcome to ask Blair and I if we know a certain spell."

"A spell that will release someone from a time bind absent the spell caster," Nessa said.

Genevieve drew her head back and shook her head. "No, I don't know such a spell, and no one I know of does, either. Is there a reason that you're seeking such a spell?"

Marlys and Nessa exchanged a look.

"That," Marlys said, "is a long story."

Genevieve lifted her chin thoughtfully. "I have a sense that I want to, no, need to, hear that story."

Chapter 24

Marlys turned to her companions. "I'll stay here for now. The rest of you, please go and browse through the library."

Serena smiled. Tir grinned. Both immediately left their chairs, extended polite thank yous to their host, and hurried out.

Rochelle stood and leaned toward Marlys. "You're certain you won't need us nearby?"

"Here, you're always nearby," Marlys said.

Rochelle nodded and left.

Nessa faced Zaria. "You may as well go, too, if nothing else, to make sure they don't find the spell we want."

"If hundreds of sorcerers here over the centuries haven't found it, chances are we won't, either," Marlys told Nessa.

"Still." Nessa waved at Zaria.

Zaria pushed her chair back and followed the others.

Genevieve pointed to Nessa, then Marlys. "I presume there is a dispute between you."

Nessa crossed her arms in front of her and leaned back in her chair. "Yes."

Marlys inclined her head slightly.

"I would be happy to moderate," Genevieve said. "I have years of experience."

"I'm willing," Marlys said, looking at Nessa.

"I don't know that our dispute can be moderated," Nessa said.

"Let me tell you what I do," Genevieve said. "I hear each of you out. You can speak as long as you wish, and the other must remain silent. I will enforce this by sorcery if necessary. Once I have heard each of you, you can then ask questions of me and each other. Then I will give my advice on how I think you should proceed. You are not obligated to take my advice, except if by rejecting it, harm will come to someone, in which case, I will intervene. Do you consent to this?"

Marlys, daughter and granddaughter of magistrates, found all this familiar. "Yes."

Nessa threw Marlys a sharp look. "I consent readily."

Marlys lifted an eyebrow, guessing that Nessa still felt that her righteous cause would be obvious to anyone hearing her out, and that, at last, she had found a sympathetic ear.

Genevieve shifted her weight in her chair so that she could face Nessa squarely. "You can start now."

Nessa launched into her story with vigor. Marlys listened carefully to be sure that Nessa did not say anything she did not already know. By the time Nessa finished, Marlys felt satisfied that Nessa had related no information that she had not heard or known already.

Then Genevieve shifted in her chair again and faced Marlys. "Now, tell me your story."

Marlys did, noticing that Genevieve pointed at Nessa a few times in the narrative when Nessa opened her mouth. Nessa remained silent.

When Marlys finished, Genevieve lowered her hand to signal the time of questioning.

Nessa glared at Marlys. "My aunt would never have stabbed you!"

Before Marlys could reply, Genevieve said, "I cast a truth spell. Both you and Marlys gave accurate reports."

Nessa pressed her lips together.

Genevieve closed her eyes and leaned back in her chair. Neither Marlys nor Nessa spoke while Genevieve considered.

Eventually, Genevieve leaned forward again. She faced Nessa first. "You are correct that Marlys has left your aunt and her cohort in a time bind for far too long."

Nessa's face showed joyful amazement.

"You were correct to bring this to the attention of fellow sorcerers. They should have helped you approach Marlys and demanded action. I can see why you felt you had to approach Marlys without them and with your only ally."

"Yes! Yes!" Nessa said enthusiastically.

"You felt this injustice so keenly that you attempted what few sorcerers have done in many lifetimes, even if it meant traveling with the one you had the dispute with, to find a solution."

"Yes! That's exactly right!"

Genevieve nodded solemnly. "I'll return to you presently." She turned to Marlys. "Did it ever occur to you, in these past twelve years, to perhaps select one or two of your former colleagues, who might be sympathetic to your cause, release them from their time-bind, and have them help you? It isn't as if you had to release all of them at a time, or none of them, you know."

Marlys's jaw dropped for a moment. She then closed it. "Uh... no, it never occurred to me."

"So now, you're in the difficult position where you will have to release them all at once, and face the disruption you know that will cause. Your dispute with Nessa could have been completely avoided."

Marlys sighed deeply, closed her eyes for a moment, bowed her head, and nodded.

Genevieve turned from Marlys to Nessa and back again.

"Are you ready to hear my advice?"

"Oh, yes!" Nessa said.

"Yes," Marlys said simply.

"My advice is for both of you to take a binding oath to release your respective time-binds at the same moment and not to cast that spell on them again."

"I would do that." Marlys saw, however, that Nessa was aghast.

"What? No!" Nessa insisted.

"It was wrong of you to put the people at Marlys's fortress into a time-bind," Genevieve said. "They had done nothing to you. You could have asked Marlys to release your aunt and the others. It is plain that she was considering it at the time."

Nessa thrust an arm in Marlys's direction. "But she was in the wrong! You said so. She hadn't released them in twelve years! How was I to think she would do so now?"

"Marlys's wrong was keeping Thorne and her cohort in a time freeze for twelve years," Genevieve said. "What your aunt and the others did was appalling. Marlys was about your age. It is clear that something drastic needed to be done to change the training methods and no one else had stepped forward to do it. She used the only method at her disposal at the time. Though it is true she couldn't tell at the beginning whether she could trust anyone in the assembly, once she had gathered and trained her own assembly, it would not have been a great risk to release one or two at time to see whether they would join her as allies. That is the only fault I can see. You are not faultless, either. Both of you need to compromise."

Nessa let out a huff, lowered her chin, and shook her head.

Genevieve slid back her chair and stood. "That concludes my mediation."

Marlys stood and faced Genevieve. "Thank you."

Genevieve gestured at Marlys and Nessa. "The next action is up to both of you."

Nessa crossed her arms in front of her and turned her gaze to the floor.

Genevieve left the room, Marlys following.

When they arrived at the library, Marlys saw Blair holding an open spell book. He seemed to be discussing the contents with Tir, who stood next to him, looking at the pages. Serena and Rochelle browsed different sections. Zaria had settled on a bench. She seemed to be absorbed in her reading.

Marlys turned to Genevieve. "Any recommendations as to where to start?"

"You seem to be the most experienced sorcerer in your group," Genevieve said as she walked. "I can point out books with more advanced spells."

"Please do."

Genevieve walked to a shelf, drew out a book, and handed it to Marlys. "This should keep your attention for a while."

Marlys accepted the book and smiled. "Thank you." She walked over to a table and sat with the book in front of her. From time to time, she glanced around to see what others were doing. Nessa eventually came in and started browsing herself.

Much later, a change in lighting caused Marlys to look up. Light from the windows had dimmed. Sorcerous light brightened.

Genevieve stood from the chair where she had been leafing through a book. "It's time for the evening meal. Since we are the only ones here, all need to help."

"Of course." Marlys closed the book in front of her and walked toward Genevieve. Her companions did the same.

When Nessa and Zaria joined them, Nessa said, "Zaria and I don't know much about cooking."

"Then you can place the table linens, plates, cups, and utensils," Genevieve said. "Fill the pitchers, set out the platters. Blair can show you."

They followed Genevieve and Blair to a large kitchen. In contrast to the stations along the spell passage, here they were all free to use sorcery to help with their cooking tasks, and did. Marlys found that the food here, as well as the food they had eaten in the inns along the way, was similar to what they ate at home.

The dining hall held enough tables to accommodate an assembly of hundreds of sorcerers. However, they all sat at a large round table ample enough for twelve.

Marlys turned to Genevieve as she pulled apart a bread roll. "Is the assembly here large enough to fill the room when all are present?"

Genevieve chuckled amiably. "No. We have 72 sorcerers and apprentices at the moment. It's rare for them all to be here at once. Much of the time, most are out in the country, using sorcery to help and heal, interviewing those who can do household spells to see whether they might have the interest and ability to become sorcerers, or simply visiting family and friends."

"In ancient times," Blair said, "there were enough sorcerers here to fill the room. There are drawings and paintings showing such assemblies. Of course, the larger meetings drew sorcerers from the entire continent, including your home, and not just the Library district."

"The sorcerous wars changed much," Genevieve added. "Decimated the sorcerer population. Separated the districts."

"But peace was achieved," Blair said, "and has lasted for years uncounted."

For the rest of the meal, Marlys and her companions asked leading questions about the spell books and their contents. Nessa and Zaria's expressions showed that they followed the conversation closely, though they said little.

When everyone had eaten, they all helped clear the table and clean up the dining room and kitchen. Marlys excused herself to go back to her room quickly, and when she returned, the others had again seated themselves at the round table with a platter of sweets in the middle. Tea and pitchers of sweet drinks were also within reach.

Marlys sat and faced Genevieve and Blair. "I wondered if you could tell me about this." She reached into a pocket and brought out the key, laying it on the table.

Blair gasped.

"Where did you get that?" Genevieve said.

"At Hilltop, along the Spell Passage," Marlys said.

"And this was just lying in plain sight?" Blair asked.

"Oh, no," Tir said. "It was hidden in a box which had been placed in a secret closet. Hilde, the current host, hadn't seen it before and said no one else she knew of had seen it before, either."

"Zaria and I never saw it," Nessa said. "Hilde never mentioned it to us, either."

"That was sensible," Genevieve said.

"Is it dangerous?" Serena asked.

"The key itself isn't dangerous," Blair said, "though it is highly spelled and responds to sorcery."

Genevieve reached out to touch the key. "This is the key to the vault we have in the caverns."

"We saw drawings and paintings of a cavern at Castlemount," Tir said.

Genevieve nodded. "Such things were left along the Spell Passage, yes. I didn't know any of the keys were."

"What's in the vault in the caverns?" Serena asked.

"A repository of spell books," Blair said.

"The spell books with our most dangerous spells," Genevieve said.

"Such as?" Serena asked.

"Legend has it there are spells there that could wreck the world," Genevieve said. "That is why no one since the sorcerous wars has ever read the books."

"Then how do you know that the legend is true?" Nessa said.

"Because we have histories of the sorcerous wars," Genevieve said. "Death on a massive scale. Land ruined and useless for living or farming. You must have seen what it is like on your approach."

"We did," Marlys confirmed.

"Do you have a key here?" Nessa asked.

"Yes, but only I and a few others know where it is or which spells to use to unlock the holding area to get it," Genevieve said.

"How do you know there is even a vault?" Zaria asked.

"Oh, that," Blair said. "We go there from time to time. We just don't open it and read the spell books."

"The cavern itself is beautiful," Genevieve said. "It's constantly illuminated by sorcery set by the ancients. It's a quiet place to sit and think, or sit and study. Our apprentices visit often."

"Can we see it?" Nessa asked.

"Yes, we can show it to you," Genevieve said.

Everyone stood.

"Shall I leave the key here?" Marlys asked.

Blair smiled. "No, you can bring it. The key is necessary to open the door to the vault, but opening it takes more than the key. There are sorcerous traps you would have to avoid."

"Traps?" Serena asked.

Genevieve nodded. "We'll show you when we get there."

Chapter 25

Genevieve and Blair led the way out of the library building and through the gate. Once they stepped onto the road, they turned to those following.

Genevieve held out an arm. "Take a moment to admire the view. Even after sunset, you can see the lights of the villages, as far as the foothills you climbed."

Marlys turned slowly from side to side. "It seems you can see the entire district from this vantage point."

"Most of it," Blair said. "It's useful for spotting fires, floods, landslides—places that are in need of sorcerous help."

From there, Genevieve started down a path around the wall which descended to a cave mouth.

Serena stepped close to Marlys and whispered, "Just as we saw at Castlemount."

Marlys nodded.

Genevieve and Blair walked inside about ten paces and stopped.

"This is a good place to look around," Genevieve said. "Note especially the fissures and holes in the cave floor. The paths inside here avoid them, but it's best to know where they are and keep away from them."

"The rock wall has bands of colors, as well as glittering crystals," Rochelle said. "Very lovely."

Tir pointed. "I see rocks along the wall with smooth tops. Places to sit?"

Blair nodded. "Worn smooth by the seats of apprentices for many lifetimes."

Genevieve again walked forward until they reached a stony arch. They saw an iron doorway had been set within it.

"There's actually a keyhole," Tir observed.

"Yes," Blair said, "the key turns and at the same time, unlocks the sorcerous spell."

"Can we try it?" Nessa asked.

Genevieve cleared her throat. "There's more to it than that." She nodded at Blair.

While the others watched, Genevieve and Blair cast spells. Marlys, who had learned many spells by observation and imitation, paid close attention. Serena also seemed to be carefully taking note.

They heard a rumble. Marlys, Nessa, and their companions all looked up and around.

"Is the roof going to fall on us?" Zaria asked nervously.

"It could if our spells were not carefully cast," Genevieve said.

Blair relaxed and faced the others. "Otherwise, it's just the cavern grumbling at us."

Genevieve turned to Marlys and held out a hand.

Marlys gave her the key.

Genevieve stepped forward and put the key in the keyhole.

As Marlys studied the motions, she felt a nudge at her arm and found that Nessa had leaned into her to get a better view. Marlys did not move or protest.

After Genevieve turned the key, she pulled the door handle. It opened noiselessly. She stepped aside. "We're not going in, but you see what's in there from here."

They crowded at the entrance. Marlys saw a small, well-lit area. Shelves lined the stone recess.

"Those are definitely spell books on the shelves," Serena said.

Blair turned to Nessa. "Satisfied that it's not just a legend?"

Nessa straightened up and faced him. "Yes." She turned and walked away toward the cave entrance, Zaria following.

Blair watched them leave. "A strange pair."

Genevieve sighed. "Yes, they have a lot to learn." She turned to Marlys. "I don't envy you your task."

"Some day the right thing to do will occur to her," Marlys said.

"But will it be sooner or later?" Rochelle said. "That's the question."

Genevieve handed Marlys the key and shut the door. They heard a click, and even more, felt a sorcerous slamming of barriers.

"You're giving it to me?" Marlys said to Genevieve.

"I have this sense that you were meant to find it," Genevieve said. "I have no doubt you will guard it responsibly."

"I appreciate your confidence," Marlys said.

That evening, as Marlys was getting ready for bed, Serena stood at the doorway.

"May I come in?"

"Of course." Marlys had the key in her hand. "I was just thinking of where to hide the key. Nessa seemed overly interested in the vault."

"I saw that, too," Serena said. "I wouldn't put it past her to try to break in."

"I wouldn't either."

Serena held out a hand. "I wanted to ask if you would let me handle the key. I found a concealment spell this afternoon that I think could work quite well."

"Did Nessa see you with that spell book?"

Serena shook her head. "No, I read it while Genevieve interviewed you and Nessa. I returned it to the shelf before Nessa came out of the room."

Marlys gave her the key. "It's yours, then."

Serena smiled conspiratorially and turned to leave, then turned back. "By the way, have you looked in a mirror lately?"

Marlys nodded. "I have. We seem to be developing auras."

"Not only that, Serena said, "when I've been practicing spells, I've noticed I can put more power behind them."

"I have, too," Marlys said. "It's wonderful, isn't it?"

"It makes every effort we expended to get here even more worthwhile," Serena said.

"I only hope we can put that power to good use," Marlys said.

"I don't doubt that we will," Serena said. "Good night."

The next morning, at breakfast, Marlys faced Genevieve. "How do apprentices awaken their sorcery here?"

"We just set them a task that's beyond their ability to cast household spells," Genevieve answered.

"How well does that work?" Zaria asked.

"We haven't lost an apprentice yet," Genevieve said.

"Of course, some try, decide sorcery is not for them, and leave before awakening their sorcerous powers," Blair said, "but anyone determined enough eventually becomes a sorcerer."

"Does everyone make it on the first try?" Rochelle asked.

Blair smiled. "Oh, no, it took me five times, but there's no time limit. Everyone is welcome to proceed at their own pace."

Marlys heard a rumbling outside. All except Genevieve and Blair turned to the windows.

"Lightning storm," Blair said as he buttered a piece of bread. "Common here."

Serena faced Blair. "Rain?"

"Sometimes yes, sometimes no," he said. "Occasionally we'll go outside just to watch the display."

"I hear a little rain," Genevieve said. "It will be good for the plants. It's been getting dry lately. Fortunately, the seasonal harvest is in."

After they cleaned up the breakfast dishes, everyone spread out through the library. Marlys could hear constant distant rumbling.

"I'm going outside," Blair said at one point. "Anyone care to join me?"

Marlys and her companions followed Blair and Genevieve into the courtyard. Facing north and a little east, they could see cloud-to-cloud lightning, as well as occasional red sprites.

"Spectacular indeed," Tir said.

Marlys heard another rumbling sound nearby and turned her head. "That's not lightning."

Genevieve also pivoted. "No, that's from the caves."

Marlys noted the absence of Zaria and Nessa. She started toward the gate. "That has to be Nessa, trying to break into the vault."

"Impossible," Genevieve said. "My key is safe."

"Ours is, too," Serena said.

"Since when has that ever stopped Nessa?" Tir said.

They all ran toward the cave entrance. Looking inside, they saw Nessa and Zaria hurrying in their direction.

"The ceiling is sagging, collapsing," Nessa said.

"What did you do?" Genevieve sounded more curious than angry.

"Well, I...." Nessa shrugged.

Blair ducked inside the entrance. "Seems to me she tried to force the vault door to open."

"I was testing a new spell," Nessa said.

"Did you not hear us explaining about the traps?" Genevieve asked, again, sounding more concerned than annoyed.

Nessa opened her mouth to answer, but before she could say anything, Blair pointed to the valley. "Wildfires!"

Genevieve took a few steps outside, then motioned to the others. "Lightning must have started them. We'll need your help."

"We have to stabilize the cave," Rochelle said.

"It will endure," Genevieve said. "Lives are at stake."

"If we don't," Rochelle said, "it could threaten the foundations of the Library."

Marlys raised a hand. "I'll see to it. The rest of you, help Blair and Genevieve."

Serena, Rochelle, and Tir started to follow Genevieve and Blair.

Behind her, Marlys heard Nessa say, "You can't leave her to that task all alone. I wasn't able to stop it by myself."

"Saving lives is more important," Rochelle said. "Marlys is well able to cast the needed spells."

Marlys heard the sound of footsteps running. She heard a grunt and glanced back to see Nessa throw back her head. "Am I the only sensible sorcerer here?"

Meanwhile, Marlys reached the vault entrance. Immediately, she sensed the trap spells, meant to protect the vault from invasion, had been breached, and now threatened to collapse the ceiling in defense. Casting counter-spells would be complicated, and she wondered if she could stop the destruction before being buried herself.

"Zaria, get out of here," she heard Nessa's voice saying. "There's nothing you can do here. We can cast protective spells to shield us."

Taking her attention from the vault entrance for a moment, she saw Nessa at her side, and Zaria at a distance close to the entrance.

Nessa wasted no time casting a blocking spell.

While Marlys continued to cast counter-spells of her own, she said to Nessa, "No, a pushing spell would be more effective. Watch my spell here and you should see where to cast."

Nessa used a hand to point up. "What about here?"

"With the rock structure, it's best to shore up the sides first and then work upward to the ceiling."

"I see it."

Marlys glanced back to see that Zaria had moved closer to them, standing on the interior path with her hands spread toward the ceiling. "Zaria! Nessa was right, you can't do anything here. Get out while you can."

"No! I can help!"

To Nessa's credit, she managed to keep generating spells while addressing Zaria. "Zaria, you'll just injure yourself again and this time we may not be able to bring you back."

Zaria threw back her head and extended her reach even more. "I know I can shore up the supports. I see them moving."

"Your household spells aren't up to the task," Marlys said while continuing to coordinate spells with Nessa. "Get out. Now."

Zaria shook her head and clenched her teeth.

Nessa shook her head as well. "I can't save her."

"She has to choose her own path," Marlys said. "There," she said to Nessa, "right there. Cast your spell when I do."

Coordinating spells required great concentration. Marlys admired Nessa's ability to keep up. "It seems we can work together, after all," Marlys said.

"I'm slowly reaching that conclusion myself," Nessa said.

"I don't expect you to be happy about it," Marlys said.

"Good. Because I'm not."

Slowly but surely, the rock walls and ceiling began to stabilize and harden.

"Let's secure it," Marlys said.

Nessa nodded. "Yes, but there's a crack snaking toward the cave entrance we have to repair."

"I have it!" Zaria called out in an agonized voice. With a cry of pain, she made an upward pushing motion and the ceiling snapped back into place. She crumpled to the ground.

At the same time, Marlys and Nessa completed their work. Marlys remained still for a moment, checking to be sure everything was holding before running after Nessa.

Nessa reached Zaria first and knelt. She put an arm under Zaria's shoulders and lifted her head.

Marlys knelt beside them.

Zaria's breathing was labored, but she seemed to be awake and alert. "I'm...a sorcerer," she managed to say.

Marlys smiled. "You certainly are." She helped Nessa get Zaria to her feet. Slowly, they helped her walk out of the cave.

When they reached the entrance, the sky had cleared. The other sorcerers were looking out over the valley.

"Still in need of help?" Marlys called.

The others turned.

"No," Serena said, "we were just checking to be sure all the fires were out."

"It took all of us," Genevieve said. "Thank you."

"How is it inside?" Blair asked.

"Everything's fine." Marlys gestured to Nessa and Zaria. "It took all of us."

Blair stepped toward them. He bent a little, putting his hands on his knees to look up into Zaria's face, since Zaria had her knees bent and head down. "I see we have a new sorcerer."

"Yes," Zaria breathed.

"I'm sure you feel like lightning struck you right now," Blair said. "Fortunately, that will pass."

"I'm counting on it," Zaria said hoarsely.

They got Zaria inside and tucked into bed. Nessa stayed at her side. The others brought refreshment, and kept checking on her throughout her recovery.

A few days later, when Zaria had regained her strength, they had a celebratory dinner. When they had eaten, Marlys gestured to Zaria to rise and stood next to her, facing the others.

"Absent Zaria's High Sorcerer, Ilse," Marlys said, "I will assume the honor of presenting to all of you Sorcerer Zaria."

The others extended congratulations, and came over to hug Zaria or pat her on the back.

Nessa walked over to Marlys. "I am ready. I'll take an oath to release your friends if you release my aunt and the others at the same time."

"I am more than willing to do so," Marlys said.

Chapter 26

The next day, in the presence of everyone else, Marlys and Nessa pressed their right forearms together and clasped hands.

Marlys spoke first. "I swear that I will release all under my time-bind at the same time Nessa releases all under her time-bind. Further, I will not renew the time-bind spell among those currently bound."

Nessa looked Marlys in the eye. "I swear that I will release all under my time-bind at the same time Marlys releases all under her time-bind. Further, I will not renew the time-bind spell among those currently bound."

Genevieve stepped forward and sealed the oath with sorcery.

Marlys and Nessa released their grip.

"Do I say 'Congratulations?'" Tir asked.

"You can," Marlys said, "but we are not done. There are still matters that need to be discussed."

"Such as?" Zaria said.

In answer, Marlys motioned to the table. All sat. Genevieve and Blair passed around a teapot and platter of sweets.

Marlys leaned forward and folded her hands on the table. "In the first place, Zaria, you and Nessa have been banished, as you recall."

Nessa sighed.

"However," Marlys said, "I did not banish you, and can use my authority to give you the freedom of Goldenvalley."

"That's a start," Zaria said.

"You have other places to go that are not in the regions," Serena pointed out. "The Spell Passage isn't, and, of course, the Library's district isn't."

"Any of you are welcome to return at any time," Genevieve said.

"I think both of you can earn your way back to the good graces of our home area," Marlys said. "It may take time, but it can be done."

Nessa nodded.

Marlys turned to Serena, Tir, and Rochelle. "We, or probably just I, need to prepare Goldenvalley for our return. It's time to utilize the sorcerous channels again."

"Yes, we don't want Celestine and the others to panic upon seeing an end point form at our fortress," Serena said.

"I'm to cast an end point all the way to Goldenvalley?" Nessa asked.

"Or Serena or I could do it," Marlys said.

Nessa sat bolt upright in her chair. "I don't remember teaching you how to create an end point."

Marlys and Serena exchanged a look. "We watched you create multiple end points for days. Both of us learned many of our spells by watching others cast spells and deducing the technique from there."

"I suppose I should have known," Nessa said wearily.

Tir looked from Serena to Marlys. "Isn't Nessa's end point spell limited to half a day's journey?"

Marlys motioned to Genevieve. "There's another spell similar to Nessa's that Genevieve showed me. There is no distance limit."

"It's a variation of the spell that creates the sorcerous channels," Genevieve explained. "Only instead of speaking through it, you walk through it. We call it a transportation spell."

"That would have to be a powerful spell, to carry us all the way back to Goldenvalley," Zaria said.

Blair smiled. "But you are all now powerful sorcerers. Can't you feel it? I can see your auras."

They all looked around at each other.

Serena smiled. "Yes, we've noticed. It's wondrous."

"I remember the moment I first saw my own aura in the mirror," Rochelle said. "An amazing feeling."

"I've watched as our auras appeared and grew in brightness." Marlys took a breath. "It's satisfying to see."

Tir leaned back in his chair and placed his hands behind his head. "At times, I just sit and let it soak in."

Nessa sighed. "I've been busy reading the spell books. I noticed the auras and returned to my studies."

"I'm new to this." Zaria shrugged. "I don't have a way to measure whether the strength of my sorcery is average or extraordinary."

Serena faced Marlys. "Going back to the issue of our return to Goldenvalley, what do we need to tell Celestine, besides the message that we're coming home?"

Marlys gestured to Nessa and then herself. "They need to prepare for our releasing our time-binds. For Isador, Skye, Bronwen, and Fern, they need to be told that their wedding will be delayed. For Thorne and company, they will experience the greater shock of awakening after twelve years. I will be older, and the current Goldenvalley assembly will be surrounding them. I will need to explain that."

"That will be no easy task," Tir said.

Marlys nodded. "To ease their adjustment to our current circumstances, I will ask Celestine to instruct the assembly to set aside rooms for those in the time-bind."

"Lucky for us that the Goldenvalley fortress is so large," Rochelle said.

"They will also have to gather the personal effects that we stored over the years of each individual, and place them in their rooms so that they will have something familiar to return to," Marlys said.

"That will require travel to the various training sites," Serena said.

"I'm sure our assembly can handle it," Marlys said. "For Thorne, she had a small suite of rooms. Her bedroom is as she left it and I placed her other personal items there. Mine are in another room in the suite."

"Thoughtful of you," Nessa said with a note of sarcasm.

Marlys turned to her. "I really wasn't planning to keep her and the others in a time-bind forever. I just didn't know when."

Nessa waved a hand dismissively.

Rochelle took a deep breath and exhaled slowly. "I presume that means we stay here a few more days while Celestine makes the preparations?"

"You're welcome to stay as long as you need to," Genevieve said.

"Thank you for that," Marlys said.

Serena smiled. "That means more time to search the library's treasures."

"You can come back at any time if you feel your research was incomplete," Blair said.

"We may do that," Marlys said. "For now, I need to explain our plan to Celestine. Go ahead and resume your Library searches. I'll join you presently."

A few days later, they stood in the courtyard, packed and ready to go. Genevieve and Blair stood to one side as the others gathered around Marlys to cast the transportation spell.

"May the blessings of the Bright Beings go with you," Genevieve said.

"And with you. Fare well until we meet again." Marlys cast the spell.

They stepped through to Goldenvalley's audience room. Marlys heard a cheer as they emerged. The end point closed.

Celestine looked at Marlys and her companions closely. "You're right. There is an aura around you."

Tir smiled. "Benefits of travel."

Marlys put down her packs and looked around. "Thank you for your welcome. I appreciate your efforts in my absence."

"We're ready," Astrid said. "Each of the time-bound individuals has one of us at hand to reassure them and answer questions."

Celestine took a step back and gestured. "We left Thorne to you, of course."

"Of course." Marlys stepped closer to Thorne's frozen form.

Nessa, meanwhile, had made her way to the to-be-wed couples. She drew questioning looks as she moved, but no one spoke to her. Marlys felt relieved: Celestine had briefed them well.

When she reached her destination, Nessa faced Marlys and raised her arms, in preparation for casting the releasing spell. "Ready?"

Marlys raised her arms as well. "Ready."

"Now." Nessa cast her spell. The two couples moved and breathed.

At the same time, Marlys cast her releasing spell. Thorne and the rest of her own assembly filled their lungs with air for the first time in twelve years.

All was quiet as the released parties took a moment to fully come to life.

Here is where it begins, Marlys thought.

To find out what happens next, read Book 2 of The Chronicles of the Library of Sorcery, *Clash of the Sorcerers*. A QR code with the link is below. More details about this series can be found at libraryofsorcery.com.

For progress reports and notifications, please subscribe to the author's newsletter at joanmarieverba.com.

Author's note: The Prologue of this novel is a highly condensed version of my short story, "Revenge, Denied," which was published in 2012. This gives a more detailed account of Marlys's journey from apprenticeship to sorcerer. For more information about "Revenge Denied," go to my website at https://joanmarieverba.com

QR code for *Clash of the Sorcerers*.